MAYA AND THE COTTON CANDY BOY

MAYA

AND THE

COTTON CANDY BOY

By

JEAN DAVIES OKIMOTO

Endicott and Hugh Books

MAYA AND THE COTTON CANDY BOY

Copyright © 2011 by Jean Davies Okimoto

All rights reserved, including the right to reproduce this book, or portions thereof, in any form. Published by Endicott and Hugh Books, Burton, Washington. www.endicottandhughbooks.com

Publisher's Cataloging-In-Publication Data

(Prepared by The Donohue Group, Inc.)

Okimoto, Jean Davies.

Maya and the cotton candy boy / Jean Davies Okimoto. -- 1st ed.

p. ; cm.

Summary: Newly arrived from Kazakhstan, twelve-year-old Maya Alazova resents the way her mother babies her brother, but when she leaves her English Language Learner program for mainstream classes and has to deal with a boy, a bully, and conflict at home, she finds her brother can help with their new culture in ways their parents can't.
Interest age group: 009-012.
"A portion of this novel appeared in the short story 'My Favorite Chaperone' Jean Davies Okimoto in the anthology 'First Crossing: Stories about Teen Immigrants', ed. Donald Gallo, Candlewick Press 2004, paperback 2007."--T.p. verso.
ISBN: 978-0-9823167-4-0 (hardcover)
ISBN: 978-0-9823167-5-7 (pbk.)

1. Teenage immigrants--United States--Juvenile fiction. 2. Minority teenagers--United States--Juvenile fiction. 3. Bullying in schools--Juvenile fiction. 4. Brothers and sisters--Juvenile fiction. 5. Family problems--Juvenile fiction. 6. Bullies--Fiction. 7. Brothers and sisters--Fiction. 8. Family problems--Fiction. 9. Young adult fiction, American. I. Title. II. Title: My favorite chaperone.

PZ7.O415 May 2011
[Fic]   2011922481

The text in this book is set in 13-point Adobe Caslon.
Book design by Masha Shubin

LCCN 2011922481

Printed in the United States of America
10 9 8 7 6 5 4 3 2
First Edition

A portion of this novel appeared in the short story "My Favorite Chaperone" © Jean Davies Okimoto in the anthology *First Crossing: Stories about Teen Immigrants*, ed. Donald Gallo, Candlewick Press 2004, paperback 2007.

For Norm Rice

TABLE OF CONTENTS

Preface

*M*aya and the Cotton Candy Boy takes place in 1994, which is the year my husband and I visited Kazakhstan. At that time our daughter, who is an English teacher, was teaching in Kazakhstan and she and her husband lived for a year with a family in Almaty. When we visited her, I was struck with the beauty, hospitality, and rich culture of the Kazakh people.

The Republic of Kazakhstan is a huge country. It is actually larger than all of Western Europe. For centuries it was populated by nomadic tribes, but in the 1700s people from their neighbor Russia came to settle there. By the 1850s all of Kazakhstan was part of the Russian Empire. In 1917, the Russian Revolution broke out and for many years there were wars and conflicts, and by 1936 Kazakhstan became part of the USSR.

In 1991, which is three years before Maya's story takes place, Kazakhstan declared itself an independent country. It is now considered the dominant country in Central Asia. The Kazakh people speak both Russian and Kazakh. In

Kazakhstan there is freedom of religion and, for the most part, there is harmony between the followers of Islam and Christianity and many other religions.

After I visited Kazakhstan, I wanted to write about a Kazakh character and decided to combine it with my deep admiration for families in many parts of the world who come to a new country and face so many challenges. The result is *Maya and the Cotton Candy Boy*.

Maya and the Cotton Candy Boy

Maya Gets a Partner

Nurzhan was pretending to be sick again. It was the third time in three weeks and Maya wanted to strangle him. She knew it was a big fake too, because she slept right next to her little brother and he'd made no sound the whole night long. Well, maybe a few little sighs, but that was all. She did not hear one tiny peep, chirp or squeak—that boy slept soundly like an old cat lying in the sun. But first thing in the morning, as soon as he hears their Mama's alarm clock ring, Nurzhan begins to cough.

Mama's clock: *RING! RING!*

Nurzhan: *COUGH! COUGH!*

The cough gets louder with each ring and Maya starts to tell him "stop faking you silly boy" when their mother bursts into the bedroom. A worried look covers Mama's face like the darkest rain cloud. *Oh my poor baby. My poor little one is sick. Cough cough* goes Nurzhan. But the person who was sick was Maya. She was sick of her mother getting tricked and then Nurzhan staying home from school because it meant he would get further behind his work and then her mother would command, "Maya, teach your little brother." And for many hours she would have to help him catch up and then what about her own life? It might be her second year at Beacon Middle School but it was only the second week that Maya had been moved into regular classes from the classes for kids who needed to learn English. And in spite of being in these mainstream classes, every morning it was the same: when Maya climbed the steps of the schoolbus, it seemed more like she was boarding a space shuttle to take her to a strange planet than riding the bus to middle school.

Maya took a seat toward the back of the bus and put her books down next to her to save the seat for Shannon. Shannon always got to the bus stop at the very last second— every day without exception. And as usual, just as the driver was about to shut the door, Shannon came tearing around the corner, charged up the steps into the bus, and flew to the back where she plopped down next to Maya.

"Whew! That was pretty close." Shannon laughed. Even all red and out of breath, Shannon Lui was beautiful, Maya thought.

"Hey, did you get the permission slip signed?" Shannon asked.

"I'm afraid I—uh, I forgot again." Maya looked out the bus window; she hated telling this lie, especially to Shannon. Maya had known about the Seventh Grade Skate for many weeks and each night she took the slip home thinking, "Tonight I'll have the courage to ask Mama and Papa to sign it." And each morning she returned to school with the slip in her pocket where it stayed, as if it had been stuck there in cement.

"Will you see Kevin today?" Maya quickly changed the topic to Shannon's latest favorite subject, Kevin Ellis, a guy in her science class that Shannon was extremely interested in. She had pointed him out to Maya outside of their PE class last week and Maya had to admit she didn't really understand what Shannon thought was so wonderful about him, but she knew people had different taste in all kinds of things. For example, Shannon liked pizza with pineapple and Canadian bacon and Maya thought it tasted terrible.

"I don't have science today, but I'm trying to figure out his schedule so I know which hall to take so I can sort of bump into him." Shannon looked around the bus. "Where's Nurzhan today?"

"He's home watching TV," Maya said, glumly.

"Your Mom lets him do that?" Shannon couldn't hide her surprise.

"He's pretending to be sick. But he says he learns things from TV. Maybe he does learn some little thing, but TV doesn't teach you to write and he can hardly write and he's in the fifth grade."

"You sound kind of mad." Shannon rummaged in her purse and took out a comb and began combing her hair.

"He doesn't like school because his English is not good. But the more he stays home, the more lost in the woods he gets. So, who has to help him with his homework all the time? Me, of course. Then after I help that stupid boy, I have to do my own work and then it's time for bed. I hardly ever get to watch TV."

Shannon ran the comb through her thick, shiny hair and then put the comb back in her purse and spread her fingers, lifting them through her hair to make it puff up.

"He's lucky to have you to help him."

"It's just expected."

The bus pulled up to the school and Shannon stood up. She was tall and slim and so pretty, Maya thought that she truly could be a model. Kids always said things to Shannon about being so tall and she would explain that *Po-po*, her Gramma, said she's tall because her ancestors came from Northern China where many people are tall. Shannon's great-grandparents came to the United States from China, and her parents spoke perfect English, not just at their jobs—but at home too—and Maya looked up to Shannon in every way.

"I'll see you in gym, Maya—and don't forget the permission slip again!" Shannon waved and bounded down the steps of the bus.

"Oh, I won't!" Maya tried to sound casual and cheery, but the truth was she didn't feel that way at all. Time was running out for her. That morning in homeroom, right after Mr. Horswill took attendance, he held up a piece of paper. "The permission slips for the Seventh Grade Skate have to be in tomorrow. And be sure to bring the slip with your $5.00 because no one's going to be allowed on the bus who hasn't gotten in both their money and their slips. Mr. Foster told us at staff meeting yesterday, he is absolutely firm about this. No excuses, no exceptions."

Maya chewed her lip, which is what she did when she was upset. She tried not to, but like people who bite their fingernails, she found it was very hard to stop. Last year when Maya was in sixth grade, her Mama and Papa wouldn't sign a single permission slip. Her mother said she thought the school was wrong to have parties after school when students should be doing their work. To her parents this party was a shallow, unimportant thing, and even though Maya knew it was not a matter of life and death, still, to her it was something very big. It wasn't just about the party, it was about whether her parents would let her be like other kids, especially now that she was in mainstream classes. And that wish was one of the biggest things in her life. If they kept refusing her this, she knew she wouldn't really die, but it felt like she would be washed away in a sea of sadness.

If she could just think of some reason the Seventh Grade Skate was educational maybe her parents would let her go. She would have to think hard. Maya thought a good time to concentrate on this would be during journal writing in Language Arts. But as soon as Maya got to Language Arts that morning, Ms. Coe said they wouldn't be writing in their journals.

. "Today we're beginning a new project," she announced, "we'll improve our understanding of world geography and use the internet for some of the research." Then she told them they were supposed to research any country other than the United States and would be working in pairs. "I've assigned partners and you'll cooperate and collaborate on the research, the writing, and the class presentation."

Next she read from her seating chart who would be partners, but she didn't get far in naming many pairs, because people began shouting. Maya still found this hard to understand. At her school in Kazakhstan teachers were always the authority, always respected. When she first went to school in America she was shocked at the way kids and teachers were so friendly with each other, and how some kids were rude to teachers. But it was also a surprise the way the teachers wanted students to do their own thinking—even to question things. Not just memorize. The teachers acted like each student had thoughts which mattered, even though they were just kids. This amazed her.

Ms. Coe waited patiently while everyone shouted.

"What's the topic?"

"Oh, man..."

"How come we can't have three people?"

"I want LaShonda for my partner."

"That's too much work for just two people!"

Maya didn't know how Ms. Coe did this, but she always got everyone to pay attention without screaming. She laughed, then she waited for quiet. She had a special way of looking at the class, then after a while they would shut up.

"Kathleen Offord and John Tam, Alan Babcock and Shamika Carter..." There was a lot of screeching of chairs and shuffling so Ms. Coe gave the look again. "Wait to go to your partner until I finish or you won't be able to hear me." Ms. Coe kept giving them the look until things got quieter, then she read more names. "Angie Nelson and Dara Hatch, Maya Alazova and Daniel Moran, Elizabeth Fierro and James Wilson..."

Daniel Moran. Maya felt her face catch on fire. She hated it when that happened and it was happening more and more. She knew she now looked like a bowl of beet soup, like borscht. Was she supposed to go to his table? Or wait for him to find her? She hadn't been in the class that long and she was sure he didn't know who she was. But there was no doubt about who he was. Everyone knew Daniel Moran. He was handsome, in fact, he looked a lot like a guy who could be in movies. A boy movie star. He had sparkling blue eyes, very shiny black hair, broad shoulders and a beautiful, bright, dazzling smile. He was funny and friendly and although it was mysterious to Maya why some people were popular and others weren't, she knew without a doubt that Daniel was popular. Hyperbole was a spelling word they had that week and Maya thought it was not hyperbole to say that Daniel Moran was the most handsome and popular boy in the class.

Since she didn't know what to do, Maya dropped her pencil. Sometimes she did things quickly without thinking. She would just do something and not know why. Dropping the pencil was like this. She felt foolish, but leaning over to pick it up was as close as she could come to hiding under the table—which was what she wanted to do. Most of all, she wanted to disappear, so she couldn't be seen, like a *prizrak*, a ghost.

"Hey? Where's Maya Alazova?"

Maya heard him trying to find her. Then someone accidentally kicked her pencil and it rolled into the aisle between the tables. She crawled after it and when she stood up, there he was, only inches in front of her.

"Are you Maya?"

"Yes, I'm Maya." Her voice stuck in her throat and the noise she made was something between the honk of a goose and the croak of a frog.

Daniel asked again. "So, you are Maya, right?"

Maya nodded.

"Okay, Maya," he smiled. "So what d'ya want to do?" He half leaned and half sat back on the desk. Leaning on things must be cool, Maya thought, so she copied him and half sat on the table, too.

"I don't know."

"What's your last name again?"

"Alazova."

"That doesn't sound Chinese." He looked puzzled.

"It's not."

"So is your Dad something and your Mom's Chinese?"

"We're Kazakh." Daniel gave her the same blank look everyone did when she said this.

"Kazakh?"

"My family came here from Kazakhstan."

"Oh yeah, near India."

"That's Pakistan."

"Oh, I know. Where there's camels and stuff."

"Well, not exactly."

"Hey, let's do that!"

"Pakistan?"

"No, that place you said. " He sat down at the table and

opened Maya's world geography book. "Show me where your family came from," he looked over and smiled at her, "for our report."

She slid into the chair next to him and he pushed the book between them, looking at the map, while she tried to find Kazakhstan. His head was close to hers and she couldn't concentrate. The countries swam in front of her: tan, yellow, brown, and green blurring with the blue of oceans.

"Is it in Europe?" He tried to be helpful.

"Not exactly." Maya stared at the map. After a moment, the countries blurred less and she saw it. "Here." She pointed on the map, filled with relief. "Here is the city we came from. Almaty. See? There...Kazakhstan."

"Oh yeah. It's in Russia."

"Well, not anymore. It was never part of Russia. It was one of the Soviet Republics and then it broke away and now we—uh—" Maya paused, feeling mixed up for a minute before she continued, "I mean 'they'—then it broke away and now they—they have their own country."

"Cool." He looked at the map more closely. "It's pretty near China. Is that why you look Chinese?"

"I don't know exactly. But Kazakh people look Asian."

"Your name sounds sort of like Russian."

"It's a Kazakh name."

"Cool." He smiled at her and her face burned again.

"We won't have to get a lot of books, you can just tell me about Pakistan—"

"Kazakhstan."

"Right. Kazakhstan. And then we'll just write down what you say and that'll be the report." He grinned, then looked up at the clock. "Almost time for the bell. I better get my stuff."

When the bell rang, Maya was relieved that class was over. Talking to Daniel had made her so nervous. But as she left Language Arts and went down the hall, she began to feel less tense. And as Maya calmed down, it started to sink in what had happened. *Daniel Moran.* She said his name to herself and started to feel a little glow, like the pink light of dawn at the beginning of a new day. *Daniel Moran.* Maya couldn't believe it. She knew he was just being friendly because he was a friendly sort of person. He'd probably never talk to her outside class, but still just the idea of being with him filled her heart. *Kak zamechatel'no* are the Russian words to describe this and she spoke these words to herself. How wonderful. *Kak zamechatel'no.*

Maya felt like she was in a dream and when she got to her locker, for a minute she couldn't even remember the combination. Finally, the numbers came to her and she opened the lock and was reaching up to put her world geography book away, when someone touched her.

"It's great you know all about Afghanistan, Maya."

Even through her thick sweater, she could feel the warmth of his hand on her shoulder. She stared with her borscht face, stunned. He was there. Daniel Moran was at her locker, and his hand was on her shoulder. He was talking to her—outside of class!

"You know, the report. About Afghanistan." He seemed to think Maya hadn't heard him.

"Kazakhstan," she mumbled.

"I'll get it right." He laughed and leaned back against the locker next to hers. "Don't give up on me."

"Okay." That was all she could think of to say.

"Hey, Dine!" he yelled to someone down the hall. Then he took off, sprinting toward the library.

Maya got her books for her next class and was closing her locker when Shannon came up. She had a big grin on her face. "How do you know Daniel Moran?"

"He's in my Language Arts class."

"Well, he sure was flirting with you." Shannon looked at her as if they shared a secret. The only problem was, Maya didn't know the secret.

"No he wasn't. He just wants me to do all the work." The minute the words tumbled from her mouth, Maya knew it was right. It was the only explanation.

"What work?" Shannon asked as they walked toward the gym.

Maya explained about the project. "See, he's just trying to get on my glad side—"

"Your glad side?"

"You know, be very, very nice to me."

"Oh," Shannon laughed, affectionately. "I think you mean to say, 'get on your good side.'"

"Yes. Good side." Even though Maya had had five years of English at her school in Kazakhstan and had been in English Language Learner classes for two years ever since her family came in 1992, there were still so many things she confused. But Shannon was always kind when she corrected her, which helped Maya to not feel so stupid.

"Daniel's lazy, you've got that right. I've known him since elementary school and I don't know if he really tries at school. Not like his older brother. Mike Moran's brilliant and a great basketball player at Franklin and even more handsome than Daniel. He's this total star and Daniel's the clown in the family. He's also a big flirt. Believe me, he was flirting with you."

"He wants our report to be on Kazakhstan since I already know about it, that's all."

"That's not the only reason he was looking at you like that."

"No." Maya shook her head. "Only the report."

"You don't know how awesome you look, Maya." Shannon raised her eyebrows and grinned. Then she hurried down the hall, calling over her shoulder, "I've got to get to my locker. See you in PE."

Awesome. Maya knew this was a compliment, but it was hardly how she thought of herself and even though she appreciated the compliment, it made her feel strange. When she looked in the mirror all she saw was a dark-haired nervous girl with big eyes like a frightened animal, a girl who looked Chinese but wasn't—a girl who wasn't allowed to do things other kids could do. Like the Seventh Grade Skate. She checked the pocket of her coat to make sure the permission slip was still there. Would she have the courage to ask them to sign it tonight? Sometimes she thought the slip would burn a hole in her pocket, because it seemed to smolder there like a dangerous thing that could cause an explosion in her home. It could make her parents blow up. Especially Mama.

Maya pulled out the slip, stared at it a few minutes, then carefully folded it and put it back in her coat pocket. At least this morning something special had happened, and she had not imagined it. Daniel Moran was her partner in Ms. Coe's class, he truly was, and she was sure that her happy feeling would last the rest of the day—at least until she got home from school and had to help Nurzhan. Nothing could take it away.

SQUASHED LIKE A BUG

It was hard for Maya to believe that Daniel could be the slightest bit interested in her, Shannon had to be wrong. But still, just the thought of such a thing was amazing. It filled her heart with joy, although she had to admit that it was not exactly a clear and smooth joy. It was like the joy had a little pimple, because way down deep, there was something about Daniel Moran that bothered her. But unlike a pimple, she couldn't put her finger on it. It was a confusing feeling and she was glad she had PE next, because PE was the one place at school where things were not complicated. All week they'd been doing gymnastics, which Maya loved, and it was also the only class she had with Shannon— which made it extra special.

Shannon was already in the gym by the time Maya changed into her gym clothes. They waved to each other across the floor as their PE teacher, Ms. Buckman, took the roll and then told them to count off by twos and get into pairs.

"Each number 'one' should pair with the 'two' on her

right." Ms. Buckman pointed to Maya and the girl next to her. "Maya and Nadine will demonstrate spotting each other for back handsprings."

Nadine Slodky stood next to Maya looking cool. Maya didn't know how a person looked cool in gym clothes, all she knew was that Nadine did. With her extra-bright blonde hair, she looked like a very famous old movie star, Marilyn Monroe—a movie star even Maya and her family knew about in Kazakhstan. And Nadine even had a little mole near her mouth like Marilyn Monroe.

"Come up here, girls," Ms. Buckman motioned to them. Nadine strolled over to Ms. Buckman and Maya followed her. Nadine stood with one hand on her hip and Maya started to copy her, but she felt dumb with her hand like that so she dropped it and just stood there.

"Nadine, you will spot for Maya, like this," Ms. Buckman positioned her arms in front of her. "Put your arms in front, like so, and plant your feet firmly on the floor. The spotter's job is to hold the gymnast in the center of her back and help her spring over." Then she motioned to Maya, "All right, Maya, I'll spot you now to demonstrate."

Maya stood a few feet away and faced the wall. Then Ms. Buckman blew the whistle. "Quiet, class! Pay attention, you'll all be doing this in a minute. Proper spotting is the way to avoid injury!"

Then someone yelled, "If I get injured, I'll sue." Everyone

started laughing, so Ms. Buckman blew the whistle again. "Settle down, girls! Maya, ready?"

Maya waved her hand to signal she was ready, then she leaned back and sprung over. She felt Ms. Buckman's hand on her back and it lifted her higher. But the truth was Maya could spring quite high on her own. She'd been doing gymnastics since she first went to school in Kazakhstan. She absolutely loved gymnastics.

"Beautiful, Maya, beautiful." Ms. Buckman patted her arm. "Now you try it, Nadine."

"A handspring, or spotting?"

"Spot first." Ms. Buckman demonstrated how to place her hands and Nadine positioned herself the way Ms. Buckman showed her. Then Maya did another back handspring. "Perfect, Maya. Good spot, Nadine." Ms. Buckman blew her whistle. "All right, class, move toward the mats and take turns with your partner. Remember, the spotter should only give the amount of lift that's needed."

"Okay, you ready?" Nadine planted her feet firmly on the floor and held her arms out to spot Maya again.

"Isn't it your turn?" Maya asked.

Nadine put her hand on her hip and sneered. "I can't stand this crap."

"Gymnastics?" Maya didn't know what she meant.

"When in my life am I ever going to need to know how to do a back handspring? Get real."

Ms. Buckman was moving around the gym going from pair to pair. Then she saw Maya and Nadine doing nothing and came over.

"Maya, you spot Nadine now."

"Okay." Maya held her arms out.

"Go ahead, Nadine." Ms. Buckman stayed next to them, watching.

Nadine sighed in disgust, then she fluffed up her hair, held her arms out in front of her, and arched her back. She stood poised on her toes with her chin jutting toward the ceiling.

Maya held her as she tipped backwards, but then she felt her arm begin to go down, inching lower and lower no matter how hard she tried to keep it up. Nadine didn't have any spring. She flopped back against Maya's arm and it collapsed like a tree branch in winter bent under the weight of snow.

"Up and over, Nadine!" Ms. Buckman stuck her arm under Nadine and pushed her over. "Good!" Ms. Buckman said, as Nadine got over. But then Nadine's heels slid out and she went splat on the mat.

"Thanks a lot!" Nadine glared at Maya and mouthed something that Ms. Buckman didn't see because her back was turned. Maya was sure it was a bad word.

"Tweeeet!" Ms. Buckman blew the whistle. "Five more minutes, girls, then head for the lockers." She turned back to Maya and Nadine. "Nadine, I want you to spot Maya and watch how she does it. She nails them perfectly."

Nadine groaned as she got up, then she stood glaring at Maya again with her arms ready. Maya turned around facing the wall, wishing so much Ms. Buckman hadn't complimented her. Then Nadine said something under her breath. Maya was afraid she was calling her a name, but she wasn't sure. Often people said words that Maya would pretend she understood when she really didn't. But this was one time instead of pretending she did understand, Maya pretended she didn't notice. But her concentration was ruined because as she started over backwards, she was off balance.

"Oh no!" Maya toppled sideways, toward Nadine. "*Spravka!*"

"Watch out!" Nadine yelled. "Yiiiiiiiikes!"

"OH NO!"

SPLAT! Maya flattened her. Nadine was smushed on the floor like a pancake with Maya sprawled on top of her. Maya scrambled to untangle her legs from her body as fast as she could.

"I apologize. I am so sorry. *Prosti menya.*"

"Oh my God, my contact! My contact's gone." Nadine poked all over her eyelid, then she got on her hands and knees and began feeling around the floor. "Help me look, you jerk. It's all your fault!"

Maya got down on her hands and knees and started looking, carefully feeling the floor.

"TWEEEEET!" Ms. Buckman blew her whistle. "That's it, girls!"

"Oh great, now what am I going to do?" Nadine whined.

Just as she said that, Maya thought she saw a little plastic thing. A little round clear plastic thing. With great care she moved over to it and picked it up. "Is this it?" Maya asked, holding it out to Nadine.

"Oh my God!" Nadine stared at Maya's hand.

"*Chto?*"

"Speak English, you dork," Nadine hissed.

"Sorry, is this your lens?"

"This *was* my lens. You've ruined it! You squashed it when you fell. It's worthless now." Nadine held out her hand. "Give it to me. At least I can show my mother what happened to it."

Maya dropped the squashed lens in the palm of Nadine's hand as Nadine looked at her with hatred in her eyes. "My mother's going to kill me," she snarled, then stomped off to the locker room.

Slowly Maya stood up. Everyone ran by her going to the locker room and she stood in the middle of the gym like a statue made from stone. All she knew was that she didn't want to be anywhere near Nadine Slodky and since

Nadine went to the locker room, there was no way Maya would go in there.

"Maya, what's wrong?" Shannon came over quickly, her voice filled with sisterly concern.

"*Nichego.*"

"It's okay if you don't want to tell me, but we better get going. We'll be late."

"I don't care." Maya blurted. "I don't want to go in there!"

Maya could see Shannon didn't want to leave her. But it could make her late if she stayed and Maya would feel so bad if Shannon got in trouble because of her. So with dread, feeling like a calf going to slaughter, Maya went to the locker room with Shannon. Shannon walked close to her as they crossed the gym floor, stepping around the mats, and Maya told her everything that happened.

"Then I landed on her and fell on her contact lens, too."

"Squashed like a bug."

"Yes, exactly like that."

"It was an accident, Maya." Shannon said in a kind voice. "You didn't do it on purpose."

"She acts like I did."

"Nadine Slodky is very dramatic. This year she wants everyone to call her Dine—she won't answer to Nadine. So many guys are after her, she thinks she's all that."

"All that?"

"It means the greatest. But I happen to know her life isn't that great."

"It isn't?" Maya couldn't hide her surprise. "But she's so popular!"

Shannon lowered her voice to almost a whisper. "My mom's cousin manages the apartment where Nadine lives." Shannon looked around to make sure no one could hear them. "Her dad was a fisherman in Alaska and he broke his back or something awful. Her mom's gone all the time, working a lot of double shifts and our cousin says the Dad yells and screams at everyone all day."

"I feel terrible."

"The contact thing was an accident, Maya. Besides, Daniel cheers her up."

"Daniel?"

"Daniel Moran, your flirty LA partner. They're going together. I think he's fascinated by her big chest—some boys are so dumb."

Maya gulped. Maybe that was the pimple on her joy.

Anxiously, she followed Shannon into the locker room. Only a few girls were left; one was putting on lipstick and the others were combing their hair in front of the mirror. Maya was incredibly relieved to see no sign of Nadine, but she was still shaking inside like a dry leaf in the wind. What if Nadine's mother makes me pay for the contact lens? Then my parents will kill me! Last week in Ms. Coe's class when they learned the word hyperbole, they had also learned the difference between the words "literally" and "figuratively," and Maya knew her parents would literally not kill her, but it would be so hard for them to get the money and she'd feel so ashamed, that she thought she would almost want to be dead.

Shannon and Maya parted outside the gym and Maya left for her health class. As she passed the English Language Learner classroom, Maya glanced in and saw Ms. Chan smiling sweetly at everyone, just like she did when Maya was in that class. Maya knew the school thought her English was good enough for her to be in mainstream classes, but English would always be her second language and as far as she was concerned, she still needed help. Most of all, it was safer there and Maya wished she could have stayed.

The bell had rung by the time she got to health class and Mr. Foster was just closing the door. Maya scurried to her seat, happy that she'd made it. She had only been late to class a few times and found it very embarrassing because everyone stared when the late people came in. She also thought this class was very embarrassing. Health. Mr. Foster taught science as well. Maya guessed that's why he was also the health teacher, but she felt very strange having a man teacher talking about some of the things they were supposed to learn. But at least for the past few weeks it hadn't been about bodies and reproduction; now they were focusing on emotional health and were doing a unit on violence. Trying to teach people not to be violent. Maya hoped Nadine Slodky had health this semester and would be paying attention.

This week they were on Unit 3: Managing Anger. Yesterday there had been a class discussion about nonviolent solutions to tense or angry situations.

"We're going to have some role playing now." Mr. Foster announced. "We'll act out the situation we discussed yesterday."

Then people started shouting and Maya wondered if the day would ever come when students shouting would seem the normal thing and she wouldn't find it surprising.

"Hey which sitch-yoo-way-shun? Ha-ha! Which one?"

"Hey, me! I'm ready for TV!"

"I want to be an actor."

"The one about the basketball?"

"Yeah, which one, man?"

Mr. Foster got everyone to shut up, then he picked three guys, David Pfeiffer, Dan Klein, and Tyler Lee, to be the actors. Tyler Lee sat next to Maya and was a very shy guy. He kept his head down and looked at the floor while he got out of his seat and went to the front of the room. Maya was relieved she hadn't been picked, but she also felt bad for Tyler because he went up there like he was on his way to get a tooth pulled.

Maya found it hard to pay attention to the role playing. All she could imagine was a tense or angry situation where Mrs. Slodky would be screaming at her to give her the money for Nadine Slodky's contact lens. Maya's nonviolent solution to this tense and angry situation would be to run away.

"Give us the money, you terrible girl!" says Mrs. Slodky.

"Yeah, give us the money, you witch!" says Nadine Slodky.

"You'll pay for this!" says Mrs. Slodky. "We'll punish you!"

"Pay up or we'll call our lawyer. We'll sue your family for every dime they have," says Nadine.

That's when Maya runs. She runs down the hall with them chasing her, but she is too fast for them. She flies out of the school, running faster and faster. Soon she finds a secret meadow behind Burger King, filled with flowers, and no one can find her. Her dog is there waiting for her. He is a good and loyal dog; his name is Soldat, which means soldier in Russian, and he loves her always. No matter what happens, Maya thinks, Soldat loves me.

Literally, there was a dog named Soldat. He was young when Maya had to leave him in Kazakhstan. He was only six months old and he stayed behind with Maya's best friend, Aina Ergepova, and now he lived with Aina and the

Ergepova family. Maya missed Aina and Soldat so much when she first came. In fact, she missed everything about Kazakhstan, even things that weren't so good there, because at least they were familiar and she knew what was going on, while everything in America was like a mixed-up mystery.

When her family first arrived, Maya wished she could talk to Aina all the time, but the truth was, the longer she was here, the less and less she thought about Aina. Maya used to be able to picture her friend so vividly, but now she couldn't. Aina had dark hair and dark eyes like Maya, but her face was hazy when Maya tried to imagine it.

But it was different with Soldat. Even though she had to leave him in Kazakhstan, Soldat was alive in her heart and in her mind. Maya thought of him all the time, and he was grown up now. He was very beautiful: big and strong, brown like a Russian bear, and whenever she needed him, she could imagine him clearly.

Maya was dreaming of Soldat when the bell rang. More good fortune, she thought. Class was over and she never got picked to be one of the actors in the role playing. She hated when she was chosen; she found it very embarrassing. Maya thought Tyler Lee probably felt that way, too, but she wouldn't really know for sure because he never talked, except to say "hello" in a shy but friendly way.

"How'd we do, Maya?"

Maya thought that sounded like Tyler, but she had to

turn around to be sure. Tyler looked at her for a minute and Maya noticed that his ears were turning quite red, then he looked at the floor. Tyler was not the kind of guy Shannon would say was really cute and awesome and a hottie, all the other things she says about popular guys. And Maya was certain he was not a popular guy because she was very sure you have to talk to be popular.

"Good. You were good, Tyler." Maya smiled. She wanted to say something kind to him, since he always said "hello" in a very nice way. But telling Tyler he was good was actually a small lie, because Maya hadn't been paying attention. She had been too busy running away from Nadine and her mother.

Maya hurried down the hall toward her locker. At the end of the hall, a bunch of eighth-grade boys charged around the corner. One guy had on a black Raiders jacket and the hood was pulled down over his face. Maya didn't know how this boy could see where he was going and she quickly scooted out of his way. He was like a giant, she thought; he was at least six feet tall, like someone who played football. Maya tried to stay away from such big people at Beacon; she was afraid she'd be run down because she was sure she was invisible to them. But soon the boys were gone, and as she was passing the gym, Maya saw a friendly face. It was Ms. Buckman walking directly towards her.

"Maya, I'm glad I saw you. Ms. Coe and I would like to talk to you. Could you come to her room tomorrow a few minutes before school?"

"Yes," Maya answered immediately. Maya thought if Ms. Buckman had said, "Maya, please go to the cafeteria and get a bowl of green Jell-O and dump it on the principal's head," she would've also answered "yes" automatically. That's because Ms. Buckman was a teacher and it was automatic for her to obey a teacher. But why did she want her to go to Ms. Coe's room before school? It had to be the contact lens! What else could it be? But why Ms. Coe? Maya became frightened and her stomach felt like a knot with pins sticking in it, and she chewed on her lip until it hurt.

On the bus going home, it was all she could think about. When she tried to have other thoughts, they would just leap to her other problem: her parents and the permission slip for the skating party. Shannon didn't notice that Maya was deep in her thoughts because she was excited about Kevin, the guy in her science class, and chattered on and on about him the whole time. At the bus stop, as Maya said good-bye to Shannon, she suddenly realized why Ms. Coe needed to talk to her. It was because Nadine told Daniel Moran about her and he refused to have her for a partner for the world geography project. "I'm not going to be partners with that dork!" he'd tell Ms. Coe defiantly. That had to be it.

When Maya got home, Nurzhan was right in front of the television still in his pajamas. It was too early for their mother to be home so he didn't move. When he heard Mama coming, he would turn off the TV and race to his bed. Then when she opened the door he'd begin coughing.

Maya went to their room, put her books down, and got the notebook she used for journal writing for Ms. Coe's class. The journal wasn't an assignment to hand in—Ms. Coe only wanted them to practice writing every day and they could write whatever they chose.

Maya took the notebook to the bathroom and locked the door. She didn't want to speak to Nurzhan, who was totally involved in TV anyway. She sat on the floor with her back against the wall across from the tub. As Maya wrote, she heard the toilet flushing in the apartment above her. Then a minute later, all she heard was the steady drip of the faucet in the bathroom sink. The sink had a stain of rust under the faucet that was shaped like a fat snail. Sometimes Maya also thought it looked like the sink was in a terrible fight and had a deep wound.

Monday

This was a strange day. Maybe the most strange day in my life that I remember. The most handsome boy is my partner and we're going to write a report about Kazakhstan. This made my heart fill with happiness. Then Shannon saw this boy (D.M.) talking to me at my locker. She said he was flirting with me. I can't believe such a thing, but it's very exciting even though I must admit there is something about him that bothers me, although I'm not sure what it is. But I was so happy until gym. Then I fell into Nadine Slodky and ruined her contact lens. Now my heart is filled with fear. Especially since Ms. Buckman said Ms. Coe wants to see me tomorrow. I wish I could stay home and pretend to be sick like that stupid boy Nurzhan.

I don't know why the teacher wants to talk to me and I'm most afraid. And I'm afraid to ask Mama and Papa to sign the slip for the skating party. If I don't have the slip tomorrow I can't go with my class. But I must ask. I must find a way to ask Mama and Papa. I want to be like everyone else.

Permission Slip...Now or Never

Maya lay awake waiting for Papa to come home. She was sure she couldn't ask about the skating party unless he was there or she'd be wasting her courage on nothing. If I only ask Mama, Maya thought, she'd say "no" automatically. She wouldn't think about it—not even one second. Maya knew the lives of her parents were very different from each other in America. Her mother was a house cleaner and the people she worked for usually weren't home, so all day there was never the sound of a voice, just the vacuum cleaner. And it was the same on the few nights a week she worked cleaning offices. There was no one there. For Papa it was not like that. Driving his cab, he talked with his American passengers and learned about things here. Maya wished Papa would learn that it would be okay for her to go to the skating party.

She was starting to doze off, when BANG! she heard a loud noise. Through the haze of sleep, Maya thought Nadine Slodky had flung open her gym locker and was about to stuff her inside. She woke quite frightened and opened one eye, then the other, and peeked over the covers as she looked around the room. Under the crack in the window shade, the orange light from the Mini-Mart sign across the street blinked on and off and she could see Nurzhan in his bed, deeply asleep. Nothing ever troubles that boy, she thought.

Then Maya heard talking, and now fully awake, she realized the noise had been Papa slamming the door. Mama was waiting for him with his dinner; she always cooked for him. Maya had observed how different this was from Shannon's house. Shannon's father cooked sometimes and he even washed dishes! Maya couldn't believe this when she first saw it; no Kazakh man would ever do anything in the kitchen. Even though their family was in America now, her father was still like that. He didn't do any work in the house, just his work outside the house, driving the cab. He came home around nine or ten every night. Then he left at six in the morning and he was always in a hurry and there was never time to ask him anything. Maya watched the Mini-Mart sign flash on and off, reminding herself that if she waited until morning, her father would be gone and all she would hear from Mama would be "no." *Nyet.* This was the moment. She had to act now.

Maya got out of bed, making sure in her mind that her dog Soldat was at her side. He'd go with her to the kitchen and stay next to her as she asked Papa and Mama to sign the slip. Soldat is a big, big dog, she reminded herself. He looks strong and fierce, but his brown fur is soft and his large dark eyes are clear and true. Soldat would never hurt me. He would do anything for me, he loves me so much. Sometimes he scares people because he appears so fierce, but his heart is kind and good.

As Maya went toward the kitchen, she heard Papa laugh. What a good sign, she told Soldat. Papa sometimes told funny stories about the people who rode in his cab. Maya thought Papa liked people more than her mother did. He was friendly, but Mama was shy. Her parents both took English classes on Thursday night at the community center. Her mother was better at reading words, but her father was better at speaking. Maya was sure this was because he always had to ask the people in his cab, "Where to?" and talk to them. And talking was also his nature.

Maya leaned her cheek against the top of Soldat's broad head, then took a deep breath and entered the kitchen.

"Papa? I have a slip from the—"

"Maya. Go to bed. It's late." Mama waved her away.

"Yes, Mama. But I have a slip from the school which must be in tomorrow."

"What is this slip? Why did you wait so late?" Mama put potatoes on Papa's plate.

Papa smiled. "She can sit for a minute, Gulnara."

"Then get your robe." Mama sat at the table across

from Papa. "But don't wake Nurzhan," she hissed. "And get your slippers."

Even though they lived in America now, they still had many pairs of slippers by the door and took off their shoes inside. Sometimes Papa left on his shoes like Americans, but Mama didn't like this. She wanted things in their home to be like they were in Kazakhstan, even though here all the streets are paved and there are sidewalks and grass. Next to the slippers near the door, they also had a *kamcha*. It looked like a small riding crop with a carved wooden handle and a braided leather rope attached to it. The *kamcha* they brought from Kazakhstan was about two feet long, one foot for the handle and one foot for the cord. It was also decorated with some horse hair. It was an old Kazakh tradition to put the *kamcha* inside the house next to the door because it was believed to bring good fortune and happiness. Maya touched the *kamcha* for luck, then pulled the permission slip from her coat pocket and scurried into the bedroom to get a pen and her robe and slippers.

As she tiptoed toward her backpack to get the pen, Nurzhan rolled over. Oh no. That boy better not wake up. That's all she would need. Mama would be angry and Papa wouldn't stay in his good mood. Maya tried to move like a cat, placing each foot like a soft whisper against the floor as she got the pen, then her robe and slippers. As she left the room she looked at Nurzhan. Good. That stupid boy's still asleep.

Maya sat across from Papa, with Mama between them, and held out the slip.

"The school must have this for tomorrow."

"What is it?" Mama frowned.

"Parents must sign this," Maya said quietly.

"But why, Maya? Why?" Her mother cut the chicken on her plate, moving her knife back and forth pressing down hard.

The only sound was the clinking of Mama's knife. Maya kept the pen in her lap, and asked Soldat for courage as she handed the slip to Papa. "It's for the seventh grade activity."

"Activity?" Papa glanced at the slip, although Maya knew he couldn't read it. "Everyone in the seventh grade is going, Papa. It's the skating party. Shannon is going."

"Shannon goes. Good. Shannon is a good girl."

"She's Chinese, Aibek," Mama muttered as she chewed her chicken.

"Don't bring old wars to new country, Gulnara."

Her mother was afraid of Chinese people from when they lived in Kazakhstan. The border of China was so close, for many Kazakh people there was always fear China would make war with them. Maya had explained to her parents that Shannon's family had been here for four generations, but Mama still put them in a box in her mind marked

"Chinese," and this box was filled with fear. Maya thought her mother was like a tree that couldn't bend in the wind. It was different with Papa. He seemed to understand that Shannon's family had nothing to do with Kazakhstan.

"Can I go, Papa?"

"All your teachers will be there?" he asked.

"Oh, yes." Maya clutched the pen in her lap. "They come with us on the bus," She breathed very deeply, she knew she was chewing her lip, but she couldn't stop. "And the bus and the activity costs all together $5.00."

Papa smiled and reached in his pocket. He took out his wallet and pulled out a five-dollar bill. "Shannon goes, right?"

"Yes, Papa."

"Okay, Maya. I sign this. You go with class. It's okay."

Mama put her fork down and folded her arms across her chest as Maya handed the pen to Papa. He signed his name, then gave her the slip. There it was, Papa's name, *Aibek Alazova*, signed right on the line. She could go with the others! Seeing his name, Maya could hardly believe such happiness. She could go!

"Oh Papa, thank you."

"It's late. Get to bed." Mama's voice was tired. Maya knew her mother didn't like this and especially didn't like Maya being given money. But Papa had decided, and what Papa decided in their house was how things would be.

Maya went back to her room with Soldat at her side. What a good dog. He had helped her be brave to ask Papa. Now, she thought, if only he would help me tomorrow when I find out from Ms. Coe what bad thing has happened. But no matter how terrible it could be, it couldn't destroy her happiness about going to the Seventh Grade Skate. Maya put the permission slip in her notebook as if it were a sheet of gold. Then she snuggled down in her bed next to Soldat, her brave, good dog.

MS. COE GIVES THE NEWS

Papa was gone when Mama rushed in their room the next morning to wake Maya and Nurzhan. Whap! She yanked up the window shade next to Maya's bed. "Get up, Maya."

Then her mother sat on the edge of Nurzhan's bed. "Nurzhan, my little one," she spoke sweetly, "are you well, today?"

Maya didn't want to lie there and listen to that stupid boy do his fake coughing. She got up and hurried to the bathroom to shower. As soon as Maya turned on the water she became very awake. Cold. Very cold, like freezing rain as it sprayed against her skin. This often happened in their apartment in the morning. Once Maya told Papa she didn't like it freezing cold. When she said that, he grunted and his jaw twitched. "Maya, it is not brown," he said, firmly. In Kazakhstan the water was often brown. They couldn't drink it and had to boil it on the stove. But the longer she was in America, the more she forgot these things. But Maya still remembered some good things that she liked, such as sitting down and having tea together every day. She

missed that. Here they were all going in different direc-
tions and everyone was very busy. She also missed pomegranates in the salad that they had for special occasions.
She loved that salad, with beets and potatoes and beautiful
pomegranates scattered over it, sparkling like rubies. Once
her mother found pomegranates in the grocery store here
but they were very expensive and she said, "Even if I could
buy, we have no special occasion."

When Maya got out of the shower, Mama came in.
Maya clutched the towel around her, trying to stay warm.

"Nurzhan will go to school. Help him with his work
after school. Then make dinner, Maya. I work late tonight."
She said nothing about the skating party. It was as though
Papa signing the slip hadn't happened. Her mother started
to leave, but then she stopped and looked at Maya, who
felt uncomfortable as Mama stared at her. "You are like
woman," she said quietly. Then she left for work.

Why did Mama have to say that? Maya didn't mind her
body changing but she didn't want anyone to speak of it.

"Maya, get out! I have to go!" Nurzhan banged on the
door.

Maya clutched the towel around her and yanked open
the door. "So! You're going to school for a change?"

Nurzhan looked a little embarrassed as he flew past her.
Maya went to their room and got dressed. It didn't take
her long because she only had a few clothes and it was

never hard to decide what to wear each day. When she first became friends with Shannon she was amazed to see how many clothes Shannon had. Then she became even more amazed when she learned that Shannon and her mother and sisters all wore each other's clothes. Maya could not imagine wearing her mother's clothes, even if she would allow it. Maya thought they were baggy and plain and had no style, not like Mrs. Lui's. Maya quickly got dressed, putting on jeans and the purple sweater she'd gotten at Nordstrom Rack for three dollars. Someone had tried it on and left a small lipstick mark on it, which is why she thought it was so cheap. Maya cleaned the lipstick and when she wore it with her good jeans it was her best outfit.

Hurrying to the kitchen, Maya put the water on to boil for kasha, then put bowls and spoons on the table. Nurzhan was dressed in one second, he never took a shower and the only time Mama made him was when he got muddy from playing outside. Nurzhan slid into his chair and began gobbling the kasha. Like an animal that boy eats, Maya thought, slopping and slurping everything all over the table.

"Don't slurp like that, Nurzhan."

"Yes, I can eat the way I want. You're not Mama."

"Then clean your own dish," Maya snapped, and took only her dish to the sink. "I'm leaving for the bus."

"Wait!"

She stood by the door and tapped her foot. "I'm not missing our bus because of you. If you are not ready in one second I'm going to..."

"I'm ready!" Nurzhan ran from the kitchen and grabbed his jacket from the closet.

"You left your bowl on the table."

"I'll clean it." Nurzhan turned and started back to the kitchen.

"Forget it! We'll be late." Nurzhan spun around and ran out behind her. Maya locked the door. "Do you have your key?"

Nurzhan felt in his pockets, and shook his head. "Why must I have it?"

"Because I might have to stay late." She unlocked the door and Nurzhan went back in to get his key. "And put your bowl in the sink!" she commanded, watching to make sure he did this. There's no reason he has to be such a baby.

"First you tell me to, then not to—what am I supposed to do?" he whined.

"Oh, just put it in the sink and hurry up." On the way to the bus stop Maya didn't speak to Nurzhan. She didn't want to tell him about why she might not be home after school. She didn't want him to know she was afraid Ms. Coe was going to give her a punishment, like detention. There wasn't anyone in her family she could tell.

All the way to the bus stop, Maya held her fear inside

while Nurzhan flitted around her like a little fly, buzzing with silly chatter. He jabbered on and on about all the things he wanted to buy, special shoes like an NBA player wears, and electronic gadgets and games of all kinds. Nurzhan had a friend who had all these things and he wanted them too.

Shannon came running up just as the bus got there. She never missed the bus, but she always got there at the last second. Being almost late like this would make Maya very nervous; she'd be afraid she might miss the bus. But Shannon wasn't like this, Maya thought. She was relaxed about everything and Maya wondered what it would be like to be this way and not have worries.

Shannon lived a few blocks from the bus stop in a nice brick house. Maya loved going over to Shannon's house. It was spacious and the water was always warm when you wanted. It surprised Maya how many people had their own houses in America. A whole house, just for one family! In Kazakhstan most people lived in huge apartment buildings with old creaky elevators. It also surprised her how people lived in so many different kinds of housing in their part of Seattle—all within just a few miles. Next to beautiful Lake Washington there were huge houses, which Maya had been shocked to learn were also just for one family. Then the houses got smaller, and then smaller as you got farther away from the lake. After that, all along

Rainier Avenue there were apartment buildings and also some public housing.

Maya's family was on the list to get into public housing. They would be able to get more room than they had now—for about the same money, but her father said it would be many years before they got to the top of the list.

One of Nurzhan's friends, Jesse, arrived at the bus stop and he and Nurzhan immediately began jumping around and punching each other and shrieking.

"I see your brother is feeling better." Shannon laughed. She knew what Maya thought about Nurzhan's illnesses.

All the way to school, Shannon talked about Kevin. Part of her plan was to hang around Kevin's homeroom and then casually bump into him, so when the bus pulled up to school, Shannon got off quickly and ran ahead to put her plan into action.

Maya walked up to the school alone. She went down the hall alone, and then stood outside the door to Ms. Coe's room alone. She felt like a fish swimming upstream about to be eaten by a grizzly bear. She had recently seen fish eaten this way on the Discovery Channel and as she stood outside Ms. Coe's door she saw fish after fish flinging themselves up a waterfall into the jaws of the bears. To find her courage and to stop thinking about the fish, Maya closed her eyes and tried to picture Soldat.

"Oh, Maya. Good."

Maya opened her eyes. It was Ms. Coe calling to her, coming down the hall from the main office. "Perfect timing." She smiled as she opened the door to her room. Maya thought Ms. Coe's blue eyes were as calm as a beautiful lake, and her brown hair the color of a chestnut. She liked her clothes, too.

Maya followed her in the room, chewing on her lower lip, trying to think hard that Soldat was next to her and not bears.

"Well, Maya," Ms. Coe began.

Maya chewed her lip and waited, thinking she should have invented a cough like Nurzhan's and stayed home.

"We're starting something new this spring in the sports program and we'd like you to be part of it. We're going to have a girls' gymnastics team."

It seemed to take some time for Maya to understand these words, but after a few seconds she did and the relief made her whole body feel loose like a rope that had suddenly been let go after being pulled very tight. This news from Ms. Coe was happy news! It was good! Maya was filled with so much happiness, it was hard to concentrate on the rest of what Ms. Coe said.

"I'll be coaching, and we'll have meets with all the other middle schools. Do you think you can be on the team?"

Maya couldn't find words, she could only nod.

"Great. We'll need your parents to sign the permission

form." She handed Maya a green sheet of paper. "Have them fill this out. It needs to be back by Friday and then we'll start practice next week."

Maya stared at the paper, chewing her lip. Her spirits sank like a balloon that had suddenly popped. Another permission form. Another mountain to cross.

"We'll practice Mondays, Wednesdays, and Fridays."

"But how late will it be, this practice?"

"Until 4:30." She looked concerned. "Is that a problem?"

"I will miss the bus."

Ms. Coe smiled. "There's the late bus, the activity bus for people who do things after school. It comes about 4:45."

"So I can ride home on this late bus?"

"Absolutely." Ms. Coe put her hand on Maya's shoulder, "just hand in the slip by Friday."

Maya nodded then rushed down the hall to her homeroom, reminding herself that she had crossed one mountain—Papa gave permission for the skating party—surely, this new mountain was smaller…maybe more like a hill. After all Papa liked sports very much. In Kazakhstan, he even coached a basketball team. And gymnastics was a sport.

All during homeroom Maya thought only of belonging to this team. She'd have teammates and they'd wear leotards all the same, purple and gold, the school colors. And in the meets, people would shout hooray when she won and then she'd go to the Olympics and they'd say, "First

place for the United States of America....Maya Alazova." Everyone would clap and cheer; it would sound like
thunder in the stands. And she'd be on the top step and
they'd play the *Star Spangled Banner* and she'd bow her
head as they placed the gold medal around her neck and
she'd hold a beautiful bouquet of flowers. Mama and Papa
would be in the stands, crying and waving. They would be
so proud.

COTTON CaNDY BOY

Maya was hoping they would have journal writing in Language Arts and she could write about the gymnastics team, but Ms. Coe wanted the class to work on their reports.

"Get together with your partners, people. We're going to spend the whole period on this. You should start by making an outline of the topics you'll cover in your report."

"Can we go to the library?"

"Hey man, my partner's sick. What do I do?"

"What d'ya mean topics?"

People started yelling out and moving chairs around and before Maya knew it, Daniel was next to her. She couldn't believe how close he'd pulled his chair, and how he leaned over with his elbow on the desk, resting his chin on his hand, staring at her.

"You want to write the stuff down, Maya?"

"Okay." Maya tried to sound casual as she took a sheet of paper from her notebook. She noticed Daniel hadn't brought his books or notebook.

"So what are some topics about Pakistan?"

Maya started to laugh. Was he really this stupid? Or just pretending to be, trying to make a joke? Oh my, if he was this stupid—she shouldn't be laughing at him. Maya covered her mouth. But as she held her hand in front of her lips, still laughing because she couldn't help it, all of a sudden she knew what it was about him that had bothered her. Daniel reminded her of cotton candy. Last semester, the eighth grade sold cotton candy to raise money for a class trip. She loved that cotton candy. She bought it with some of her lunch money and ate it even though it was just sugar and probably bad for her. It was a big, fluffy, sweet mass on a paper cone—but it disappeared almost immediately. Daniel Moran seemed like that. He was a cotton candy boy and even though somehow she knew it—Maya couldn't help liking being with him. It was exciting and he was so much fun.

"What's funny?"

"Kazakhstan. Not Pakistan." Maya smiled, she didn't want to tell him about the paper cone under his head.

"Oh yeah. Right, sorry." He leaned closer to her. "Write that down for me, will you?"

On the top of the paper in big letters Maya wrote "K A Z A K S T A N." Then she wrote it another way, "KAZAKHSTAN."

"There are two ways it is spelled," she explained.

"Why's that?"

"I don't really know, I think at first they left out the "h" to make it easier for foreign people, then they put it back. I think they decided it didn't matter so much about the foreign people."

"Okay, well let's make it easy and choose the shorter one."

Maya nodded and crossed out "KAZAKSTAN" and left the shorter one. But then it bothered her, so she crossed it out and spelled it with the "h".

"It's only one letter longer. We'll spell it this way."

"Whatever." He leaned even closer to her and slid the paper over so it was between them. "Ka-zakh-stan," he said slowly. "Okay. I got it. So what are some topics?"

"I'm not sure about that." Maya really did have an idea, but there was part of her that doubted herself and she didn't want to say and be wrong. But there were many things to tell about Kazakhstan. How there used to be tribes who roamed the land and lived in yurts, and it was an important place on the ancient silk road where traders went from China to Europe, and almost everyone now in the whole country could read and write, and religion was a free thing. You could believe what you wanted to believe and it was a huge country, even bigger than all of Europe. And then there was tea. Maya missed how her family would have a slow, quiet time and drink tea and have a little bit of bread.

Not everything rush, rush, rush. Sometimes their neighbor Mr. Taeneva would join them and he played the dombra and the music was beautiful.

"Hey, Ms. Coe?" Daniel yelled, "is what you mean by topics stuff like how many people live there, what's the weather like? Stuff like that?"

"Yeah, what do you want us to write about?" a bunch of people yelled.

"Think about your lives. For example, go through a typical day and think about what your life is like and see how many questions you come up with about life in the country in your report."

"She never just tells us." Daniel slouched over the desk again.

"I think she means to think about things like what kind of home you have and then to find out what kind of homes the people in the country have."

"Oh, I get it, and then what kind of food they eat, and jobs they have, and stuff like that." He sat up and stretched, then he put his arm on the back of her chair. "So write down housing for the first topic."

Underneath where Maya had written "Kazakhstan" she wrote:

I. Housing

She put a Roman numeral "One" so it looked like an

outline. But something didn't seem right to her. It didn't seem to be the best place to start because they hadn't even explained where Kazakhstan was located.

"That looks good. Okay, so what kind of housing do they have there?" Daniel started drumming his fingers on the desk.

"I think we should begin by saying where it is located."

"Fine by me."

Maya erased "Housing" and wrote "Location" instead, but then she crossed that out. "I think Geography is more correct."

"Fine by me." Daniel said again. Then he opened her book to find the map of the world. "Okay, so where's it at?"

Maya was looking on the map when Daniel leaped up. "Hey, just show me on the globe." In one second he was at Ms. Coe's desk grabbing the globe next to it. "Okay?" he asked, as he was about to pick it up.

Ms. Coe nodded. Then Daniel stood back, rolled up his sleeves and grunted like a strong man who lifts weights. He acted like he was struggling and he staggered and grunted, straining as he slowly lifted it over his head. By then the whole class was laughing as he pretended to wobble under the weight of it.

"That's enough, Daniel," Ms. Coe said in a firm voice. "Back to work, people."

Daniel straightened up and carried the globe with ease next to Maya's desk.

"Now, where's that place?" He smiled, spinning the globe.

Maya put her hands on the globe to stop it spinning. She liked the feel of its smooth surface on her palms, turning it slowly past Japan, Korea, Mongolia, China, until she came to Kazakhstan. Then she pointed it out to Daniel.

"Cool. Hey, it's near Tashkent."

"How do you know Tashkent?" Maya was surprised.

"My cousin went there with her high school class. It's one of Seattle's sister cities."

His eyes sparkled when he smiled and Maya felt embarrassed to notice this. She quickly looked at the globe but her only thought of geography was "his eyes are as blue as the Caspian Sea."

"You must know the names of all the countries around there," he said.

Maya nodded. "But I'm not sure about English spelling." So Daniel spelled each one slowly and Maya wrote it down.

"Now, how about housing?" He tapped the table with his fingers again.

"But we did not explain about mountains and weather."

"So what's the weather like?" Daniel yawned.

"It is very hot in the summer and cold in winter."

"Does it snow?"

"Yes. Much snow."

"Okay, put that down. Climate, that's it, put it under climate."

As Maya wrote down about the climate, Ms. Coe looked up from her desk. "Straighten your chairs, people, it's almost time for the bell."

"Maya, give me your phone number so I can call you about the report," Daniel said calmly, picking up the globe to take back to Ms. Coe.

Her heart banged like a drum and she tore a scrap of paper from her notebook and wrote down her number. No boy had ever asked for this. Maya was sure it was only because of the report, but her heart pounded anyway. When Daniel came back, she handed him the scrap of paper and her cheeks felt hot and she knew her face was like borscht.

"Thanks." He smiled and stuck the paper in his pocket.

"Sure." Maya was too embarrassed to look at him, she looked only at the clock as if waiting for the bell.

For the rest of the day Maya's thoughts went from Daniel Moran wanting her phone number, to Ms. Coe wanting her on the gymnastic team. Back and forth between two such thrilling things! Even though Maya believed Daniel Moran only wanted her number for the report, she was still awed by this. And even though she didn't know if her parents would give permission, it didn't take away her happiness at being asked to be on the team.

By the time Maya got to computer class the two things had come together in her mind. Then, when she stood on the podium at the Olympics and looked out over the crowd, she saw Daniel Moran sitting in the stands next to her family, waving and cheering. And when Maya came down from the podium with her gold medal, he rushed from the stands carrying a beautiful, big bouquet of bright red roses with red, white and blue ribbons streaming from them. Then he picked her up, sweeping her off her feet, and he spun around with Maya in his arms and their hearts were bursting with joy.

Peanuts and Cracker Jack

On the bus ride home Maya told Shannon that Daniel asked for her phone number. "But I know he only wanted it for the report."

"Right, the report, like he's totally into that!" Shannon laughed.

"But what else could it be?"

"Duh." Shannon laughed again.

"But you said he has a girlfriend, Nadine Slodky."

"You're gorgeous, Maya. You just don't get it. He's probably going to dump her for you." Shannon held her hand out and looked at her nails. "Do you like this color? I was thinking about getting blue polish, but I'm not sure."

They talked about Shannon's fingernail polish and also a lot about Kevin Ellis and how he never seemed to be where Shannon thought when she planned to bump him.

Maya was about to tell Shannon about the gymnastic team when she heard a big commotion coming from the seats behind them.

"I do, too!"

"You do not, dumbhead."

"Yes I do!" It was Nurzhan's voice in some kind of argument. "I even know the song." Then Maya heard Nurzhan singing. *"Bring me some peenoots and creker jerks..."*

"Ha ha! *Creker jerks!!* That's right, you jerkhead!"

Maya turned around, bending her neck to see who it was. It was Jerry Hong laughing his head off about Nurzhan.

"Do you believe this guy," Jerry said to the whole bus. "He thinks he knows something about baseball. Ha! *Peenoots* and *creker jerks!* Ha!"

Then the bus came to their stop and Nurzhan ran down the aisle.

"So long creker jerk!" Jerry Hong yelled.

As Maya started to get up from her seat, Nurzhan rushed by. His head was down and his face had red patches on it. Nurzhan's face got like this when he cried.

"Jerry Hong." Shannon hissed. "He's the jerk. Tell Nurzhan not to mind him. Jerry always picks on kids he thinks are F.O.B."

"Yes. Okay." Maya left the bus and when she stepped down from the last step, Nurzhan was already past the next corner, almost out of sight down the block where the Mini-Mart was. His coat was a small dot of red blurring along the black trunks of trees.

Maya didn't know what to say to him when she got home. She felt really sad for him to be teased about the way he spoke, but she was also annoyed. If he didn't stay home so much, he could speak better and they wouldn't call him what Shannon said: F.O.B…"Fresh Off The Boat."

What did he learn from those cartoons he watched? *Bam! Screech! Crash! Pow!* That's all. But what a surprise when Maya opened the door. The apartment was quiet. No *Crash!* No *Pow!* No TV. Nurzhan wasn't on the couch in his usual place, sitting there like a turnip staring at his cartoon show. She went to their room and looked in. No Nurzhan. He must be in the bathroom, but the door was open and it was empty. Then Maya found him in the kitchen sitting at the table, staring at his book, quiet as a small mouse. He looked up at her, his eyes wet with tears.

"Ms. Kirkman taught us that song. Someone had a tiny radio on a Mariners key chain in class."

"You can't have radios in school. The teachers must take them and give them back at the end of the day," Maya said.

"I know that, so does Ms. Kirkman. But before she took it, she played the song and then she wrote it on the board so we could all learn it. It's a famous song called 'Take Me Out to the Ball Game.'"

"Shannon says that boy Jerry Hong is a jerk."

"I hate it."

"Hate what?" Maya asked.

"When they laugh."

"Go to school more, Nurzhan."

Nurzhan looked down at his book. "Help me with my work, okay?" Then he looked up. "Please?"

"Okay, but I have to start dinner."

Maya called Nurzhan that stupid boy, but she didn't really think he was stupid. After she helped him for twenty minutes and it was time for her to start peeling potatoes for dinner, he knew all the words. What was stupid about Nurzhan, Maya thought, was that he didn't try enough.

Maya cut the vegetables for the salad and washed the chicken. Mama said the chickens in Kazakhstan were thinner than here and had a different flavor, and it took her and Papa a long time to learn to like American chicken. But Maya had forgotten what chicken tasted like in Kazakhstan. She only remembered Mama pulling feathers out, not like here where chickens in the store were bare.

Nurzhan took his schoolwork to the front room and Maya set the table for dinner. While she was folding napkins and putting down the forks and knives, she tried to think of how to talk to Mama about the gymnastics permission slip.

"Mama, wouldn't you like it if I went to the Olympics for the United States of America? You would? Okay. Sign this paper."

Then Maya heard the door open. Mama was home and the first thing she said when she came in was, "Oh, Nurzhan, I see you are doing your work. What a good boy."

Then she pulled the lid off the pot where the potatoes were cooking and checked them. "Tch," she clucked her noise of disapproval. "Be more careful when you peel them. Get all the brown off."

"Yes, Mama." Maya checked to see how the chicken was cooking and thought more about how to talk about the gymnastics team. She breathed deeply, trying to be bold enough to say something. Maya took another deep breath, then turned around, but Mama wasn't there. She heard the water running and realized her mother had gone in the bathroom. After a few minutes, she came back carrying her purse.

"Read this to me, Maya." She took out a piece of paper from her purse and handed it to Maya. "Mrs. Hathaway left this on the table with my money."

Maya looked at the note and read aloud, *"Dear Gulnara, We'll be on vacation next week and won't need you to come to work. But we'll expect you the following Tuesday as usual. Thanks. Lorna Hathaway."*

Mama grabbed the paper from Maya and crumpled it, her face red with anger. Maya knew Mama thought it was wrong that Mrs. Hathaway could go away when she wanted, leaving her with no work that day and no pay. But she was afraid she would lose her job there if she spoke about it to Mrs. Hathaway. She didn't dare do this.

That evening Papa took a break and came home for an early dinner. No one talked much as they ate. Maya's parents were often too tired from working to talk and as soon as Papa finished eating, he got ready to leave.

"Wait, Papa. Please." Maya ran to her backpack and got the slip.

Papa looked at his watch. "I must go."

"Wait. Please." She ran to him and held up the slip. "The school needs you to sign your name. You or Mama."

"Again? What is it for?" Papa looked at it, then put it on the table. "So much permission, they need. All these extra things."

"They want me to be on the gymnastic team."

"Don't you do that anyway? Don't you have physical culture in school?" Mama seemed upset. "What does *this* cost?"

"This is a team, for competition. For competition with other schools."

"You have to travel for this?" Like a storm cloud, a worried look crossed Mama's face.

"I have to practice after school. There is a later bus I will take. I will be home about 5:00 on Monday, Wednesday and Friday."

"Almost every day! When will you cook? And help Nurzhan with his schoolwork?" Mama demanded.

"I must leave." Papa put on his jacket, leaving the slip on the table.

"But what about me!" Maya blurted.

"Don't speak like that to your father!" Mama's voice was like ice.

"Mama and I will talk. I will tell you tomorrow." He turned to leave.

"Papa." Maya tried to show respect. "They only ask you to be on the team if you are good. It doesn't cost any money!"

"Tomorrow," he said firmly. Then he left for work.

Nurzhan didn't fall asleep right away that night. Maya was awake, too—she often lay awake thinking about things before she could sleep. Tonight she was wondering if they would let her be on the team and then she wondered again about Daniel Moran. He probably just wants me to do all the work, she thought. But could it be more than that? Part of her hoped it was and part her hoped it wasn't. It made Maya think again about cotton candy and fighting inside herself about whether she should have it, and wanting to have it even though she knew it was only sugary fluff.

"Maya," Nurzhan whispered.

"What?"

"Will you teach me how to say the words in the song?"

"Song?"

"You know. The baseball song."

So Maya sang the song and then after a minute, Nurzhan sang with her.

"*Take me out to the ballgame,*" they sang, "*take me out to the park. Buy me some peanuts and cracker jack. I don't care if I ever get back.*"

"Nurzhan," she told him, "it's *peanuts*. You say the *eeee* sound and then *nuts*, like an *uh* sound. And *cracker*, like an *aaa* sound and *jack*."

"Not jerk?"

"No. Jack."

"What is cracker jack?"

"I don't know."

Then they sang again together. "*Buy me some peanuts and cracker jack.*"

"Maya!" Mama burst into their room. "Stop that noise. Don't you keep Nurzhan awake, he needs his rest!" Then she shut the door very hard, almost a slam.

"Sorry," Nurzhan whispered.

"Shhh." Maya lay still under the covers, waiting a long time until it was very quiet. Then she got her journal from next to her bed and tiptoed to the bathroom. She closed the door and put on the light. Maya sat on the floor and leaned against the bathtub. Under her thin pajamas, the tub was cold against her spine.

Tuesday

Mama blames me for everything. Even helping Nurzhan

62

with his song. It is not fair. She expects me to be like an adult, doing all the cooking, all the cleaning up, teaching Nurzhan, translating English for her. Then she shouts at me like I am a small child and I am supposed to be an obedient child, waiting for them to decide if I can be on the gymnastics team. If I was in Shannon's family they would understand what it meant to be asked to be on this team. They would be honored and would shout joyously and Mrs. Lui would cook for me my favorite food—hamburgers and French fries like they have at their house—and I would sit at the table and not have to cook anything myself and Mrs. Lui would say, "Congratulations, Maya!" and put the hamburger on the table.

GOOD NEWS...BAD NEWS

By the time Maya's mother put on her coat to leave for work the next morning, she still hadn't said anything about the permission slip. When Papa came home so late was he too tired to talk about anything? Or did Mama just forget? Maya searched her mother's face for some sign, but her face showed nothing.

"Did you talk, Mama? The permission slip, Mama. For the team—the gymnastics team?"

A slight smile turned up at the corner of her mouth. "Papa said I should not imprison you to potatoes if you are to become a champion."

"Oh, Mama, thank you!" Maya wanted to do back handsprings all over the apartment. But her mother's smile quickly faded, as if the sun had popped behind a cloud.

"But I said you still must cook when I work late. And when we have our class."

"Yes. Of course, I will do that."

"And you must help Nurzhan with his work."

"Yes, yes. I will."

Mama touched their *kamcha* on her way out the door and Maya watched her through the window as she hurried for the bus. She walked fiercely along the sidewalk, so serious with her head down and the collar of her brown coat turned up against her face. Maya thought her coat looked like a potato sack. She wished Mama had a bright red coat with gold buttons like Shannon's mother. But Mama said her coat was practical—she said with pride that she didn't have to worry about her brown coat looking dirty. Maya recognized that her mother was a very practical person and she was sure that was a good thing when you didn't have much money. She wasn't ashamed of her mother's coat—many mothers of the kids who had been in her English Language Learner class had the same kind of coat—she just thought her mother would look so nice in a bright red coat with gold buttons.

Her mother grew smaller as Maya watched her move into the distance, becoming tiny like a little brown bird and then finally just a speck before she turned the corner and disappeared. Thank goodness for Papa. Maya was sure if it was up to Mama she wouldn't be allowed on the team.

Why was it, she wondered, that in her family Papa seemed more sympathetic to her, and Mama to Nurzhan? Was it this way just in her family? Or did many families have such teams? With one child and one parent on one team, and the other child and another parent on the other. Like the way they chose up sides in dodge ball.

It didn't seem to be this way in Shannon's family and Maya thought she might ask her about this on the way to school. Shannon liked to explain things to Maya and give advice. But that morning, just as Maya was going to ask her about this, Jerry Hong came on the bus and when he got to Nurzhan he said in a loud voice, "Good morning, creker jerk!"

He kept it up all the way to school. Calling Nurzhan "creker jerk" over and over repeating it many times, then laughing hysterically each time.

"I heard Jerry Hong's brother is in a gang," Shannon whispered.

"Really?" Maya wondered if this was true, but one thing she was sure about was that Jerry was not a nice boy. He was mean.

"Nurzhan should just ignore him," Shannon advised. "If Nurzhan shows he's upset, Jerry will just do it more."

They weren't not allowed to get up from their seats on the bus, so Maya couldn't go to Nurzhan to give him Shannon's advice. But she could see that he didn't need her to tell him. Nurzhan was staring out the window, shutting out everything around him, as if he had pulled a dark curtain around himself and hadn't heard a word that was said by that mean boy, Jerry Hong.

Maya said good-bye to Shannon by the front door and wished her good fortune in her plan to crash into Kevin. She thought it was a good plan because if someone crashes into you, you would surely notice them.

After homeroom, on the way to Ms. Coe's room to hand in her permission slip, Maya heard voices of people arguing coming from the next hall. They were around the corner and she couldn't see them, but she was sure it was a girl and a guy yelling at each other, and the guy's voice sounded like Daniel Moran. But was it really Daniel? Maya wondered. Ever since he became her partner she had found herself looking for him in the halls. There were many times when she thought she saw or heard him, but was mistaken.

"What do you mean, you don't know?" the girl shouted.

"Because I don't, that's all." The guy's voice wasn't as loud.

"Just like that?"

"No, not just like that—it's just that—"

"Well, you know what you can do!"

As Maya came around the corner, she saw Daniel standing outside the library door with Nadine Slodky. They were so involved in their argument, they didn't see her.

Ms. Coe was in her room when Maya arrived with the permission slip and as she handed it to her, Ms. Coe smiled her lovely smile. "Our first team meeting will be in the gym today after school. It won't last too long, I'm all for short meetings." Ms. Coe laughed. "Then practice starts next week. But it's important that everyone make the meeting."

"Do I need to take the late bus?" Maya was surprised the team would meet so soon.

Ms. Coe shook her head. "I'm serious about short, it'll be only about ten or fifteen minutes. You can get the regular bus, just meet us in the gym at 3:00."

"I will be there."

Maya felt warm and happy inside to think about the team, and having Ms. Coe to be her coach. She wished Mama was a happy person like Ms. Coe. She loved thinking about getting to be with Ms. Coe three days each week after school, not just in class, and that soon she'd belong to something. It would be so wonderful to meet her teammates, to work together for the good of the team, to care for each other and cheer for each one. And they'd care for her, and cheer for her too. And they'd look so fine in their purple and gold leotards. Perhaps they'd take a photo of the team and put it in the school paper. Wouldn't that be an awesome thing!

It was almost time for the bell and Maya had to walk quickly to get to her computer class on time. Just as she reached the door, Shannon came flying down the hall. "It worked! I bumped into Kevin!" She grinned and handed

Maya a note. "Here, I wrote you all about it. *And* there's some big news. Some other big news!"

Then a deep voice boomed, "The big news, Miss Lui, is that if you don't get to class you'll have a referral." It was Mr. Haight, the vice-principal who patrols the halls getting people to class.

"I'm on my way." Shannon grinned just as the bell rang.

Maya wondered how Shannon could smile in such a calm and friendly way when she was about to get in trouble. If Mr. Haight spoke to her that way, she'd be terrified.

Maya hurried to her seat and unfolded the note in her lap. She propped the note up in front of the computer so it couldn't be seen by Ms. DePue, then put her hands on the keyboard and looked at the note as if looking at the screen.

Hi Maya,

You'll never guess what happened! Daniel Moran broke up with Nadine Slodky. I heard about it at lunch from Vera Eng. It's absolutely true! And I know why even if you don't. He wants to go with you!

I'll bet anything he makes a move soon. The skating party is coming up next Friday and then it will just be a few weeks until the dance. Kevin wore his Sonics

shirt today, he looks so cool in it. I'm trying to find out his schedule so I can see him between every class!
DON'T DO ANYTHING I WOULDN'T DO. Ha-ha.

Luv ya,

Shannon

Could Shannon be right about this? Maya had heard their argument in the hall, so that part must be right. But what about the other part? She stared again at the note... *He wants to go with you...* Surely, that must be a mistake!

But even though Maya believed this was a mistake, her thoughts of Daniel rushed wildly like rapids in a raging river. And by the time class was almost over, the river had opened to a wide lake covered with ice and she and Daniel were gliding smoothly on this silver lake, skating together in perfect harmony. His arm was around her waist and when she lost her balance a little bit, he held her strongly and pulled her close to him. Then he whispered, "I loved seeing you at the gymnastics meet, Maya. When you took first place."

When Daniel Moran said things in her mind he was the way Maya wished him to be, never silly, always strong and caring. As wonderful as Soldat—only he was a boy, not a dog. Soldat was nothing like cotton candy and in her dreams Daniel Moran wasn't either.

Maya's beautiful thoughts were broken by the sound of the door opening and closing. When she looked up, she saw Mr. Haight standing by Ms. DePue's desk. He whispered something to her and then she nodded. And then Maya was stunned because her teacher nodded and pointed to her!

"Maya, you're wanted in the office," Ms. DePue said. "You can go now with Mr. Haight."

Her fingers tingled with fear. *What was wrong? What had I done? Mr. Haight only comes for people when there's trouble.*

Like a robot, Maya gathered her books and followed Mr. Haight. As he closed the classroom door behind them, Maya's heart began to bang and she felt like she needed to go to the bathroom. In the hallway Mr. Haight told her Ms. Taylor, the school counselor, wanted to speak with her.

"What is wrong?" Her voice came out as a whisper. Maya felt such dread, she could barely speak.

"What's that?" Mr. Haight couldn't hear her whisper.

"What is wrong?" Maya tried to talk louder.

"She didn't say. She just asked me to find you since I was heading down the hall anyway."

Maya suddenly remembered Sunstar Sysavath, who was in her English Language Learner class last year. Her family came from Cambodia and on her first day at Beacon she was in the wrong line in the lunch room. Mr. Haight

71

went to help her and he tapped her on her shoulder to get her attention. When she felt the tap and saw him, she lifted her hands in the air as if she were arrested and about to be shot. People who saw this in the lunchroom laughed, but it wasn't a joke. Sunstar was filled with terror.

Maya knew she wouldn't be shot, but walking with Mr. Haight to the office seemed like one of the longest walks of her life. Lately, Maya's mind had been filled with many things—being with Soldat, competing at the Olympics, or skating at the party with Daniel Moran. And some bad things, too, like Mrs. Slodky punishing her for squashing her daughter's contact lens. But now Maya's mind was filled with nothing. It was empty, like a dry river bed where there is only cracked, baked earth and nothing lives.

She walked in the main office where Ms. Taylor was waiting. "Come with me, Maya," Ms. Taylor smiled at Mr. Haight. "Thanks, Chad."

Like a person made from wood, a puppet, Maya followed Ms. Taylor through the main office down the hall to her office across from the principal's. Ms. Taylor motioned to a chair and closed the door.

"Sit down, dear."

Maya sat in a chair across from the desk and clutched her books to her chest. She had never been in the school counselor's office before. She looked at the name plate on the desk. It said, "Rosetta Taylor." Ms. Taylor had many nice green plants in front of the window and a small fish tank in the corner. Maya stared at the brightly colored fish swimming back and forth.

Ms. Taylor sat at the desk and picked up a pink message slip. "Maya, I received a call from Mr. Burke, the principal at Evergreen Elementary, and your brother's been suspended for fighting."

"Nurzhan?"

"Yes. Nurzhan Alazova," she read his name from the slip. "They haven't been able to locate your mother, so they called over here to see if you could help."

"Is Nurzhan all right?"

"Yes. And I believe the other boy wasn't seriously hurt."

"Who did Nurzhan fight?" Maya knew it was a foolish question; she was sure of the answer.

Ms. Taylor hesitated, so Maya said, "Jerry Hong."

Ms. Taylor nodded.

"What must I do?" Maya asked.

"The suspension policy requires that the parent or guardian must have a conference at school within 24 hours of the suspension. Can you help us locate your mother or your father?"

"Yes. I can do that."

"Do your parents speak English, Maya?"

"Just a little."

"Then perhaps you could attend the meeting and translate for them."

"Yes. I must always do this for my parents. At the store, at the doctor, things like that."

"Here's the phone. You just press 9 for an outside line. I'll step out for a minute to give you some privacy."

Ms. Taylor left the office, quietly closing the door behind her. Outside the window, the sky was gray and it had started to rain. Maya stared at the phone, wishing more than anything that she didn't have to be the messenger with this bad news. But there was no choice. She knew she must do it, so she picked up Ms. Taylor's phone and called the Northwest Cab Company dispatcher and asked them to contact her father.

"Aibek Alazova. Cab 191. I'm his daughter and there is a family problem I must speak with him about."

Maya stayed on the line while they radioed Papa. She looked at the clock and felt her heart grow heavy. In a minute the bell would ring, school would be out, and the gymnastics meeting would begin.

"Maya!" Papa's voice was alarmed. "What is wrong?"

"Nurzhan has been in a fight with another boy." Then she explained in Russian what had happened and Papa said he had to drop his passenger at the Four Seasons Hotel downtown and then he'd come straight to the school. He'd be there about three-thirty.

Ms. Taylor came back in the office as Maya hung up the phone. "Did you get your mother?"

"I don't have the number where she works today, but I got my father. He will come to the school."

"Good."

"Ms. Taylor?"

"Yes?"

"I will leave now for Evergreen. Will you tell Ms. Coe I have family problem and I cannot attend the gymnastics meeting?"

"Of course. And I'll call Mr. Burke at Evergreen now and let him know that you and your father will be coming."

Maya went to her locker, got her coat, and walked to the south door, the one closest to the play field that joined Evergreen. Poor Nurzhan! Getting in such big trouble. Maya couldn't fault him for fighting with Jerry Hong, that mean boy. She hoped Nurzhan gave Jerry Hong a hard punch. But why did he have to make this fight today! The first day of my team meeting, of all days. She felt angry that she would miss the meeting because of Nurzhan. Would Ms. Coe still want her on the team?

But as Maya neared Nurzhan's school—her old school—she only worried about Papa. Even though he didn't shout at her on the phone, she knew it didn't mean he wasn't angry. He had a person in his cab and the dispatcher might have been listening. Probably the dispatcher didn't know Russian, but Papa wouldn't show his anger in the cab anyway. Papa could be very, very angry. Not just with Nurzhan but with her, too. Her parents thought it was her duty to watch out for Nurzhan and keep him out of trouble. She knew they would think she had failed at this job and as she hurried in the rain toward Evergreen Elementary, Maya was afraid.

SaVING NUrZHaN

as Maya scurried toward Evergreen Elementary, Mr. Zabornik, the custodian, waved to her. He was picking up papers and litter around the bushes next to the front walk. It was still raining lightly and Mr. Zabornik's wet gray hair was pasted against his forehead.

"Hi, Maya."

"Hello, Mr. Zabornik."

"Here about your brother, I suppose."

"How did you know?"

"I was fixing the drainpipe when it happened." He pointed to the corner of the building by the edge of the play field. "That kid Jerry Hong was teasing Nurzhan something fierce. Telling him he could never be a real American, making fun of the way he talked." He bent down and picked up a candy wrapper. "Reminded me of how my father said bullies would tangle with him when he first came here after the revolution."

"Oh." Maya said, with a blank stare. She knew Mr.

Zabornik could tell she didn't know what he was talking about.

"The Hungarian Revolution in '56." He looked out over the play field and folded his arms across his chest. "Guess some things never change."

"Nurzhan's going to be suspended."

"Sorry to hear that. 'Course the school can't allow fights, and this was no little scuffle. But I can sure see how your brother lost his temper." Mr. Zabornik turned and went back to picking up the litter. "Good luck," he called over his shoulder.

"Thank you, Mr. Zabornik."

When Maya got inside, the school looked smaller than she remembered. At the beginning of sixth grade, when she first went to middle school, she had come back to visit her old teachers. She'd also been back one other time when she came to the parent-teacher conference to translate for her mother. But Maya hadn't been inside Evergreen since last semester and it appeared the whole school had shrunk, like a shirt washed in water that was too hot.

In the front office, Ms. Jefferson, the head secretary, spoke to her in a very kind way. "Maya, Mr. Burke is waiting for you in his office. You can go right in."

That was one thing she missed about elementary school. Most of the teachers, the custodian, the nurse, and the people who worked at the school knew all the kids. Not like at Beacon, where Maya didn't know the teachers unless she had them for class. Even though Evergreen was a small place, today it was a small place with big trouble and Maya's stomach was jumpy as she went in Mr. Burke's office.

Mr. Burke was behind his big desk, and Nurzhan was sitting on a chair in the corner. He looked like a rabbit caught in a trap. He had scrapes on his hands and on his cheek, and his eyes were puffed up. Maya couldn't tell if it was from crying or being hit.

"I understand your father will be coming, is that right, Maya?"

Maya nodded, as she chewed her lip.

"Just take a seat by your brother. Ms. Jefferson will bring your father in when he arrives."

Then Mr. Burke read some papers on his desk and Maya sat down next to Nurzhan and spoke quietly to him in Russian.

"*Eto normal'no, Nurzhan. Ya tebya ne vinyu* ." "It's okay, Nurzhan. I don't blame you," is what she said.

Nurzhan nodded, his eyes wet with tears.

Maya stared out the principal's window. Across the street, the bare branches of the trees were black against the cement gray sky. The rain was coming down in a steady drizzle and after a few minutes, Maya saw their father's cab turn the corner. His cab was green, the color of a lime, and Papa always washed and shined it. Maya watched him park and get out of the cab. His shoulders were very broad underneath his brown leather jacket and Papa had a powerful walk, like a large, strong horse that plowed fields. He walked briskly and as he came up the steps of the school, he removed his cap.

To Maya, it seemed like one thousand years, but it was only a minute before Ms. Jefferson brought Papa in the office. Nurzhan and Maya stood up when he entered, but he didn't look at them, only at Mr. Burke, who shook hands with him and motioned for him to have a seat.

Papa sat across the desk from Mr. Burke and placed his driver cap in his lap.

"We have asked Maya to translate, Mr. Alazova."

"Yes." Papa nodded. When he heard Maya's name he understood.

"Your son, Nurzhan, was involved in quite a nasty fight."

Papa looked at Maya and she said to him in Russian, "Nurzhan, was in a little fight."

Mr. Burke continued. "The other boy, Jerry Hong, needed two stitches at the hospital."

"The other boy, Jerry Hong, was a little hurt," she told Papa.

Nurzhan's eyes became wide as listened to Maya's translation.

"We have a policy that anyone who fights must be

suspended from school; both boys will receive a two-day suspension."

"The other boy, who is very bad," Maya translated for Papa, "is not allowed to come to school for two days and his parents must punish him. Nurzhan must stay home, too. But he should not be punished so much."

Papa nodded.

Then Mr. Burke said, "We've been told the other boy was teasing your son. We'd like you to help Nurzhan find ways to handle this situation without resorting to violence. We're working with the other boy to help him show respect for all students."

Maya looked at Papa and translated, "The other boy was teasing Nurzhan in a violent manner. This boy will be punished and must learn to respect all students. We understand how Nurzhan became so angry and we ask that you punish him by not allowing him to watch television."

"Yes, I will punish my son as you suggest." Papa said in Russian.

Maya looked at Mr. Burke, "My father says he will teach Nurzhan not to fight by giving him a very serious punishment."

"We are glad you understand the serious nature of this situation," Mr. Burke said. Then Maya told Papa in Russian the exact words of Mr. Burke.

Mr. Burke held out a form on a clipboard. "We require

you to sign this to show that we've discussed the suspension and you'll keep Nurzhan at home until Monday."

Again, Maya told Papa exactly what Mr. Burke said and Papa signed the form.

Maya and Nurzhan said nothing as they left the school and followed Papa to his cab. They sat in the back, not daring to speak. There was a small rip in the leather of the seat and Maya poked her finger in it. The cab smelled of perfume, maybe Papa's last ride was a lady who wore a lot of it, Maya thought. It smelled like some kind of flower, but she couldn't name it. Maya wished right then that she was in a beautiful meadow filled with sweet-smelling flowers, lying in the soft grass looking up at the clouds while Soldat lay by her side. She tried to calm herself thinking about this meadow, but she just kept feeling scared. Scared Papa might somehow find out that she'd changed what Mr. Burke said. Maya thought maybe she should feel bad about changing Mr. Burke's words, but she didn't. She only felt afraid. It wasn't that she thought changing words like that was okay; she had to admit it was sort of like telling lies. But Maya thought that some lies were probably okay, like the play they read last semester about Anne Frank and how the people lied and said no one was in the attic when they really were. They lied to save the family from the Nazis. Maybe she wasn't saving Nurzhan from death, Maya thought, but she was scared of what Papa might have done to Nurzhan if she hadn't changed the words. Maya stared at the back of Papa's thick neck; it was very red and he drove in silence until he pulled up in front of their building. Then Papa shut off the engine, put his arm across the top of the seat and turned his face to Maya and Nurzhan, craning his neck.

His dark eyes narrowed and his voice was severe. "I am ashamed of this! To come to this school and find you in trouble, Nurzhan! This does not seem like much punishment to me, this no watching television. You will go to bed tonight without dinner." He clenched his teeth, "I have lost money today because of you. And Maya, you must keep your brother out of trouble!" Then he waved them away furiously, like shooing away bugs. "Go now! Go!"

They ran into their apartment and Nurzhan marched straight to the table in the kitchen with his books. He was in such a hurry to do his work, he didn't even take off his jacket.

"Take off your jacket and hang it up, Nurzhan."

"Okay."

Maya began peeling potatoes for dinner, while Nurzhan hung up his jacket. Then he sat back down at the table, "Maya, I—"

"Don't talk. Do your work."

"But I—"

"I missed the first gymnastic meeting because of you!"

"Watch the knife!" Nurzhan looked scared.

Maya glanced at her hand. She was holding the knife and had been waving it without realizing it.

"I wasn't going to stab you, stupid boy."

"I was only going to say thank you." Nurzhan looked glumly at his book.

Maya went back to peeling the potatoes. She'd had enough of him and his troubles.

"For changing what Mr. Burke said when you told Papa," he said in a timid voice, like a little chick peeping.

"It's okay, Nurzhan." Maya sighed. "Just do your work."

A few minutes before six, they heard Mama come in. She came straight to the kitchen and when she saw Nurzhan sitting there doing his work, a smile came over her tired face.

"Oh what a good boy, doing his work."

"Not so good, Mama, Nurzhan got in trouble." Maya didn't mind telling her this bad news too much. It wasn't like when she had to call Papa. Then Maya explained about the fight and how Papa had to come to the school.

"Oh my poor little one!" Mama rushed to Nurzhan and examined his hands. Tenderly, she touched his face where it had been cut. Then she turned sharply toward Maya.

"Maya! How could you let this happen?"

"Me! I wasn't even there."

"On the bus, when this boy is so bad to Nurzhan. You must make this boy stop."

"No, Mama." Nurzhan explained. "He would tease me more if my sister spoke for me."

"I don't understand this. In Kazakhstan, if someone insults you, they have insulted everyone in the family. And everyone must respond."

"It's different here, Mama."

Mama looked sad. She sighed deeply, then the phone rang and she told Maya to answer it. Mama always wanted Maya to answer because she was shy about speaking, so Maya spoke on the phone to the women her mother worked for and then would translate. She translated their exact words, not like with Mr. Burke.

But the phone wasn't for Mama. It was Shannon.

"Maya, why weren't you on the bus? Did you get my note?"

"Yes. I am so happy for you that you spoke to Kevin." Then she explained to Shannon about what had happened to Nurzhan and having to miss the meeting.

"Ms. Coe is cool. Don't worry, it won't mess anything up."

The water on the stove began to boil and Mama scowled and pointed to the potatoes.

"Shannon, I have to get off—"

"Okay, but listen. He's going to call you!"

"Who?"

"Duh. Daniel Moran. That's who!"

Mama motioned to Maya to get off the phone. "Okay, Mama. I'm about to hang up," she said in Russian.

Shannon kept talking. "I found out from Vera, she sits next to him in math. He's calling to see if you're going to the Seventh Grade Skate on Friday."

"Oh yes, I will be there! Then Maya nodded to Mama. "Okay, okay."

After she hung up, Maya closed her eyes for a moment blocking out Mama and Nurzhan, and the kitchen became an enchanted skating rink. As she went to the stove, Maya heard beautiful music and glided with Daniel Moran by her side, holding his hand. All evening she dreamed of this, although they glided around holding cotton candy. Maya wanted to get the cotton candy out of the picture, but it just stayed there. Big fluffy blobs of pink sugary cotton, like a warning sign in her daydream that wouldn't go away no matter how hard she tried to erase it. She even tried to substitute popcorn balls, but it didn't work. They just skated around and around with the cotton candy while she tightly held his hand.

Maya opened her social studies book, hoping to concentrate on homework, but instead she found herself listening for the phone, wondering if Daniel Moran would really call.

She watched the clock and with each tick there was no ring. One half hour passed, then another, then another and another, and Maya knew then that Shannon had been told the wrong thing. What a foolish girl I am! she thought. How could I have believed he would call?

It was eight-thirty when Mama and Papa got home from their English class at the community center. Papa seemed more tired than usual and Mama was tense. Maya was sure their hearts were heavy with the burden of Nurzhan's suspension. Mama and Papa sometimes argued and when Maya heard them shouting, it was usually about the kids. Papa understood that they wanted to be like other kids and do things everyone else was allowed to do. But Mama thought children in America had too much freedom. She wanted Maya and Nurzhan to only go to school or stay home with the family. The most terrible arguing was when they realized they couldn't get the kind of jobs they had in Kazakhstan. Maya guessed they thought that because they knew so much math that their English wouldn't matter so much—but it did, and finally they had to just take what they could get. Mama found her cleaning jobs first. It wasn't easy for her to do that kind of work after being a math teacher, but the worse thing was that for a while she was the only one working. Papa didn't make any money and he was ashamed that his wife was the one who earned it. "I am Aibek Alazova and I am still head of this family!" he'd shout. It got better after Papa got his job with the cab company. But tonight Maya could feel anger in the air and it brought to mind all those days when only Mama had work.

Papa went straight to the television and snapped it on. He liked to watch basketball and the Sonics were playing. Usually he got home too late to watch anything, but on the nights they had their English class he always hoped to find basketball or some other sport. He could understand the sports without having to understand what the announcers were saying.

It was almost nine o'clock when the phone rang. Nurzhan was at the kitchen table closest to the phone, so he answered it. Maya closed her eyes, listening only to the beating of her heart. Then Nurzhan stood in front of her, grinning.

"Maya, it's for you. And it's not Shannon. It sounds like a guy!"

She tried to remain calm as she walked through the front room where Papa watched the game, hoping he was paying attention only to basketball.

In the kitchen, Maya leaned against the wall, wishing she was in a phone booth with privacy as she picked up the phone. Nurzhan sat forward at the table, listening like a puppy with his ears cocked.

"Hello."

"Hi-ya, Ma-ya," Daniel laughed, "bet you think I'm calling about the report, huh?"

"I guess so—I mean, I don't know." Her cheeks felt warm and Maya knew she had her borscht face. At least he couldn't see her.

"It's the half, so I thought I'd give you a call."

"The half?"

"Sonics game. They're smokin'."

"That's nice."

"You like sports, Maya?"

"Some, I guess. I'm supposed to be on the gymnastics team."

"How 'bout skating? You like to skate?"

"I'm not very good, but I like to."

"Why don't you show me Friday? At the Seventh Grade Skate?"

"Okay."

"I'll be looking for you."

"Okay." Her heart had been pounding the whole time they talked, now it pounded louder.

"Well, gotta watch the S-u-u-u-u-u-per Sonics. Ha. Sound like the announcer, don't I? Well, see you tomorrow Maya. Bye-ah, Maya!"

"Bye." Maya rested her head against the wall and closed her eyes. *Daniel Moran had actually called.* And he wanted to be with me! With me, Maya Alazova! At the skating party on Friday! She leaned back against the wall, keeping her eyes closed, remembering his voice. She didn't want to remember it exactly because sometimes he sounded silly. Instead she saw the enchanted skating rink and in this picture Daniel wasn't talking, but acting more like Soldat. And she and Daniel were slowly gliding hand-in-hand across the silvery surface to the beautiful music.

"Maya!" Papa's voice was harsh. "Come in here!"

Papa's voice scared her from the skating rink and Maya quickly went to him.

"Who was that?" Papa snarled.

"What?"

"Who? On the phone?"

"Someone from my class, Papa."

"A boy. I heard Nurzhan say it was a boy. Is that right?"

"Yes."

"What did this boy want calling you so late at your home?" Papa's face was red and he held his hands tightly together in fists.

"We have a report we work on together."

"And he must call you at night?" Papa pounded his fist on the table. "Don't lie to me, daughter!"

Tears stung her eyes and Maya couldn't speak.

"No boy calls my house! *Nyet!*" Papa shouted. "*Nyet!* I forbid this!"

Maya Lies

The sun rises late during the winter months and it was never light when Maya left for school, but this morning as she walked to the bus stop it seemed the darkest of all days. Her heart went out to Nurzhan, who was home for his punishment, the suspension for his fight with Jerry Hong. As she got ready for school, he was sitting at the kitchen table, trying to do his work. He wouldn't watch TV like he did when he pretended to be sick, Maya knew. He'd be too scared. She did think it might be good for her brother to concentrate on his work, but she couldn't help feeling sad for him. He looked so alone, like a baby duck stuck in the weeds while his family swims away into the lake. Her father left first, then her mother, then Maya.

"Work hard, Nurzhan," she called to him on her way out. But there was no answer, not even a peep, or a quack. Maya looked back before she closed the door. Nurzhan sat with his elbows on the table, looking down at his book, but his hands covered his face.

Before Maya left, she touched the *kamcha* by the door.

She felt she needed all the help she could get to have good fortune. It was damp and cold and as she scurried along the sidewalk, Maya could see her breath in the chilly air like small clouds of mist. It seemed so odd to walk without Nurzhan. He was always next to her chattering like a monkey, and even with the cars and city buses rushing by in the morning traffic, it seemed strangely silent. Maya realized she actually felt kind of insecure without her brother, which was a big surprise because she thought Nurzhan offered as much protection as a little rabbit.

To calm herself, Maya began to think of her wonderful dog Soldat. Maya needed him so much this day to help her with her biggest problem, which had nothing to do with Nurzhan. It was the problem she'd been worrying about ever since last night. It worried her so much that she slept poorly and it worried her from the moment she got up. In the shower, she worried. Brushing teeth, she worried. Putting on clothes, she worried. Eating kasha, she worried. All the time, Maya was worrying about this one thing: how to tell Daniel Moran never to call her house again?

She got to the bus stop before Shannon. It was always that way, Maya thought. It would be a weird thing if Shannon ever got there first. As she waited for Shannon, it seemed to Maya that was the way life was: some people arrived early, some people were on time, and others arrived late and it was always the same people in each group. Do people ever change? she wondered. Can they? Could Papa change? Could there be some words she could speak that would change his mind and then it would be fine with him to have a boy call her. The phone would ring and Papa would answer. "It's for you, daughter," he would say and smile a kind smile, pleased that his daughter was such a fine girl that a nice boy would call. If only if there were some magic words that could make this miracle happen, like the magic that makes a caterpillar turn into a butterfly. If only she could find that same magic and turn Papa into a father like Mr. Lui. Shannon had told Maya that with all his daughters talking on the phone so much, he decided to have two telephones. One phone for Shannon and her sisters and one phone just for Mr. and Mrs. Lui. Maya thought this was an amazing thing when she first learned of these two telephones in the Lui's home.

Shannon came running up just as the bus came. Maya desperately wanted to ask her for advice, but it was too embarrassing to tell her that she was forbidden to have a boy call her. Even though Shannon knew Maya's family was different, she would find it unbelievable. "But Maya," she would say, "it's only a phone call. I don't get it. It's not like you're getting married," she would say.

No, Maya thought, I won't tell this problem to Shannon.

It would only make more embarrassment to speak of it and know she couldn't understand.

"Hey, Maya," Shannon ran up the steps of the bus behind Maya. "Did he call? Did he?"

"Yes." Maya smiled shyly.

"So did Kevin!"

"Really! How wonderful!"

"Is that cool, or what? He's going to meet me where we put on the skates. Are you meeting Daniel?"

"He said he would look for me—but I'm not exactly sure what that means."

"Duh." Shannon grinned. "Of course you're meeting him!"

When they got on the bus, Maya decided she would take her problem about Daniel and put it in a little box and shut the lid, hiding the box inside her mind to take out some other time. As the bus bounced along, passing the Mini-Mart and the E-Z Day Cleaner, all Maya wanted to do was share the excitement about the party and the boys who had called them. And for some beautiful moments, with the box hidden away, Maya realized she felt almost like Shannon, like a mainstream girl.

Maya avoided thinking about her problem until math class. Math was easier for her than any other subject and she liked it very much. Today Ms. Aoki showed the class new equations on the board, then handed out sheets of problems to be finished in class. Maya finished with twenty minutes left before the bell so she took her very difficult Daniel Moran problem out of its box. She had twenty minutes to decide what to tell him.

What would happen if I just told him not to call? she wondered. But then she was afraid he'd think she didn't like him. If she told him her father didn't want any boys to call, he might not believe her because this was so strange, and think she was lying to get rid of him. Or, if he did believe it, he would think Maya had such a strange family and she was so strange that he wouldn't want to be with her at the skating party or ever again.

Two minutes before the bell rang, Maya thought of something. She thought of a lie.

"Daniel," she would say, "my father must use the phone every evening for his work, so I cannot have any calls."

He might say, "You mean you can never talk on the phone?"

Then she could say, "Oh sure, after school before my father comes home is okay. But I'm on the gymnastics team so I am not home much after school."

The bell rang and Maya gathered her books, practicing saying the lie to herself when Tyler Lee stopped at her desk.

"Hi, Maya." His whole face seemed quite red—not only his ears. He looked as if he had been exercising or maybe sitting next to a hot radiator.

"Hi, Tyler."

"Maya?"

"Yes?"

Tyler looked at her in a strange way. It seemed as though he wanted to say something but couldn't. Then he looked out into the hall. "Well…see ya," he blurted, then fled from the room as though he'd forgotten something.

He was gone when Maya got to the hall. For a moment, she wondered what he wanted, but then didn't think too much more about it. She needed to concentrate on telling Daniel Moran the lie. There was nothing more important than this because if Daniel called again when her father was home, she knew her father would take away the skating party permission. She knew this would happen as surely as night takes away the day.

Ms. Coe had them get with their partners for their world geography project and as Daniel pulled his chair next to hers, Maya practiced saying the lie to herself. *My father uses the phone at night so I cannot have calls.*

"Okay, what's next, Maya?"

My father uses the phone at night so I cannot have calls.

Maya got their outline from her notebook and Daniel leaned close to her to read it. "So we've got geographical location and climate. Now what?"

My father uses the phone at night so I cannot have calls. When do I tell him this lie?

"Maya?"

"Yes?" She glanced quickly at him. *My father uses the phone at night so I cannot have calls.*

"You sure must be concentrating."

"Yes." *My father uses the phone at night so I cannot have calls.*

"So, what's next?"

Behind them Norman Schwartz and Constance Williams were looking up the population of Bolivia. So Maya said, "Population, I think."

"Good. Okay, let's put that down. So how many people live there?"

"I don't know exactly. Maybe we can look in that book Ms. Coe told us to use." *My father uses the phone at night so I cannot have calls.*

"She said we could take turns using the internet, too."

They both looked at the back of the room. Jenny Saechao and Tori Smith were using the computer that's connected to the internet. "Okay, I'll get the atlas." Daniel stood up and yawned and stretched. Then he went to the bookshelf and brought back the atlas. "Guess we'll be stuck with the old-fashioned way for a while. A lot of people are waiting for the computer," he looked at the back of the room again before he sat next to Maya and opened the atlas.

"Hey Maya, what's your email address?"

"I don't have one. I just use the computers at school or

sometimes at the library." *My father uses the phone at night so I cannot have calls.*

"Well, I've got your phone number anyway. So I'll check in with you the old-fashioned way there, too."

"Daniel," she heard herself say his name and her voice trembled, sounding nothing like the way she wanted it to, as the words rushed from her like stones tumbling down a cliff. "My father uses the phone at night for work so I cannot have calls."

"So when can you talk?"

"After school, except many days I stay here for gymnastics practice."

"You're on the gymnastic team?"

"Yes."

"Cool." Daniel smiled. Then he leafed through the atlas until he came to the index. "Spell it for me again, Maya."

"It is spelled two ways. Remember?"

"I guess I forgot." He grinned. "Why two?"

"I don't know. But like I said before, I think maybe the new way was to make it easier for foreign people. 'K-a-z-a-k-s-t-a-n' and the old is 'K-a-z-a-k-h-s-t-a-n.'" Maya smiled to herself as she spelled the two Kazakhstans for him. How easy this had been! Foolish girl, she thought, I'd spent so much time worrying when it hadn't really been that hard to tell Daniel this small lie once the words finally flew from my mouth.

Maya felt light, as if the box where she put this problem had weighed many pounds and now it had been opened and tossed away. The happiness she felt lasted throughout the day, and after the last bell when Shamika Carter, one of the most popular girls in the class, called across the hall to her, "See you at practice, Maya," she felt like doing handsprings and cartwheels all the way to the gymnasium.

aFTer SCHOOL DiSaSTer

When Maya got to practice everyone said "Hi, Maya." Besides Shamika, Maya knew the other seventh grader on the team, Catherine Johnson. But all the rest were eighth graders and she only knew one, Dana Illo, who was a T.A. in her computer class. But they all said "hi." How can I ever find words to explain how it feels to belong, she thought. They were glad I had come and they wanted me. They didn't act like I was strange or different. *They wanted me, Maya Alazova, to be with them.*

They sat on a mat next to the vault and Ms. Coe told them how she wanted them to behave.

"Gymnastics is an individual sport, but we're also a team. And the success of the team depends on the success of each individual. So there's nothing more important than to give each other support and encouragement."

Then Ms. Buckman spoke. "It's obvious when a gymnast does well, and of course then you'll congratulate her. But even more important, as Ms. Coe said, is to say 'good try' or 'you'll nail it next time' when a gymnast has tried but hasn't been as successful as she wished. There's nothing more important than trying."

Ms. Coe walked to the vault and placed her hand on top of it. "This is a sport that requires strength, stamina, discipline and most of all—courage. Remember, we ask courage of ourselves and we will *en*-courage our teammates."

"Today we'll work on the vault, but on our next practice we'll bring in the very low practice beam, as well as the regulation beam. You'll be in two groups and will switch equipment, spending half of each practice on the beams, and half on the vault.

Shamika raised her hand.

Looking at Shamika, Maya wondered what it would be like to be so confident that you could stick your hand right up and be the first one to speak.

"Yes?" Ms. Coe called on her.

"What about bars and floor exercise?"

"We'll work on those week after next. Any more questions?"

No one said anything so Ms. Coe continued. "All right then. We'll do some stretches and then begin vaulting. We'll do just the basics first: squats and straddles. For the squat, your hands are placed wide and your legs tuck through touching together, toes pointed. And straddles are with the hands close and the legs wide. These are the basics and most of you know them, but today we'll be reviewing them. After everyone had stretched, Ms. Coe blew the whistle. "Okay, line up people. Shamika, let's lead off with you. A squat first."

"And remember, " Ms. Buckman added, "those of you who are waiting in line have a job to do. You're not just standing there waiting your turn. You have something very specific and important to do. What is it, team?"

"En-courage!" everyone shouted, and Maya shouted with them.

"Way to go, team! Great shouting!" Shamika clapped and everyone laughed. Ms. Coe and Ms. Buckman laughed too. Then Ms. Buckman blew her whistle. "Okay Shamika, begin!"

Shamika stood with perfect position, her head looking straight ahead at the vault. When Ms. Buckman gave her the nod, she raised her right arm, stepped on the mat and ran very fast straight at the vault.

"Go Shamika! Go girl!" Everyone cheered.

She sailed over it but when she landed, she fell back and lost her balance, wobbling on one leg.

"Good try, Shamika!"

"Nice speed!"

"You'll nail the next one!"

As each girl went over the vault and received encouragement from the others, Maya was struck with what a nice thing this was. It was something that never happened in her family. Her Mama and Papa never said words of encouragement. It wasn't that Maya thought she wasn't loved. She knew they loved her and Nurzhan. But it was just understood that she would do her very best work, both her work at school and her work at home. She was supposed to do it. It was expected. They only spoke of her behavior if she made a mistake.

When Maya's turn came and she ran like the wind and sailed over the vault, she heard her teammates shouting, "Go, Maya, go! Go girl! You can do it, Maya! Go for it, Maya!" Their shouts rang in her ears like beautiful music, and the cheers stayed with her like the melody of a song that you keep hearing long after the last note is played. It stayed with her after practice when she went to the locker room to change, and even as she left the building to wait for the bus, Maya could still hear the music of those cheers.

She waited with her teammates outside the gym door and the girls were talking about their team leotards when two guys from the wrestling team came around the corner.

"Hey, Maya! How was practice?"

It was Daniel and Steve Shanaman, a guy in her health class.

"Hi." Maya smiled at Daniel, but then looked away, pretending to look for the bus because she felt nervous.

But he came right up to her. "Wrestling practice was

great. We worked on take-downs and escapes, then lifted weights. How was your practice?"

"It was really fun. We spent most of it on vault."

"I'm still pumped from weight training!" Daniel grinned and picked up a metal trash can by the gym door. He paraded around with the can, then set it down with a bang right next to Maya. Everyone was laughing and then Daniel bent his knees and bounced up and down on his heels and said, "Check this out Steve, am I strong or what?" The next thing Maya knew he had one arm under her knees and one arm under her back and he scooped her up!

"*Ostanovit!*" she shouted, as he lifted her. Maya grabbed him around his neck to hang on and her head was squished against his shoulder. He strutted around in a circle before he let her down. She could feel her borscht face and she flamed with embarrassment and excitement and couldn't stop laughing from both nervousness and joy.

"That's nothing, man." Steve went to Shamika and picked her up, lifting her as high as his shoulders.

Maya thought it was exciting and kind of crazy—Daniel and Steve showing each other how strong they were. First picking up her up, then Shamika, then putting them down, then picking them up and lifting them higher as if Shamika and Maya were weights. After a few times whenever Daniel picked her up, Maya was easily putting her arms around his neck. She loved being his pretend weight even though Shamika and Maya were both shrieking the whole time. Maya knew Shamika was a strong girl and if she didn't like being lifted up and held by Steve there was no way it would be happening. Maya couldn't believe it, but she began to relax in Daniel's arms and laughed each time as he slowly turned in a circle.

Then Shamika and Maya tried to pick them up and it they all thought it was hilarious. Every time the girls tried to grab them, the boys did wrestling moves on them and they ended up on the grass in a big heap, like a litter of playful puppies. They lay on the grass laughing and then Daniel and Steve jumped up and picked up Maya and Shamika again.

But this time when they turned, as Maya's face was pressed against Daniel's shoulder, she saw something coming toward the school which made her tremble with fear.

"Daniel, please. Put me down!" Maya's voice cracked and her breath caught in her throat.

But Daniel didn't hear, everyone was shouting and laughing and he held her, turning slowly in a circle as the lime green cab came to a halt in front of the school. The door slammed. Papa stood like a huge bull in his dark leather jacket and flung open the back door of the cab.

"MAYA ALAZOVA!" His voice roared across the parking lot. He pointed at Maya like one might identify a criminal. "*IDI SYUDA*!" he shouted in Russian. COME HERE!

Daniel dropped Maya and she ran to the cab, whimpering and trembling like a dog caught stealing a chicken.

Papa didn't speak. His silence filled every corner of the cab like a black cloud slowly suffocating her with its dark rage. Maya held tight to Soldat, putting her arms around him, pressing her head against his soft fur. He sat steady on the seat, still and strong, never thrown from side to side as she was, as Papa furiously sped around corners. And his proud head never jerked like hers when Papa slammed the brakes to stop at a red light. Papa's neck was deep red and the skin on the back of Maya's hands tingled with fear. She lay her head back against the seat and closed her eyes, squeezing them shut while she held tight to Soldat and took them far away until she was safe on the bars at a beautiful gymnastics meet in the sky. While Soldat looked up at her, Maya swung back and forth, higher and higher, and then she released and flew to the next bar through fluffy white clouds as soft as goose feathers, while the air around her was sweet and warm, and Soldat joyfully barked and her teammates cheered for her, their voices filled with love.

They screeched to a stop in front of their building. Maya's head slammed back against the seat, and when she struggled from the taxi it was as though she had fallen from the bars, crashing down onto the street where she splintered into a million pieces. And as hard as she tried, Maya couldn't find Soldat and get back on the bars any more than she could stop the hot tears that spilled from her eyes. Papa roared in front of her, and as he charged toward the door in his glistening dark leather jacket, he again seemed transformed to a creature that was half man and half bull.

"Gulnara!" He flung open the door, shouting for Mama, his voice filled with anger and blame.

"Why are you here? What has happened, Aibek?" Mama came from the kitchen as Nurzhan darted to the doorway and peeked around like a little mouse.

Maya closed the front door and leaned against it with her wet palms flat against the wood like a prisoner about to be shot. She closed her eyes so she could see Soldat standing in front of her guarding her with his very life.

"Is this how you raise your daughter! Is this what you teach her? Lessons to be a toy for American boys!" Papa spat out the words.

The color rose in Mama's face like a flame turned up on the stove and she spun toward Maya her eyes flashing. "What have you done!"

"Your daughter was in the arms of an American boy."

Mama looked shocked. "When? H-How can this be?" she stammered.

"Outside the school as I drive by I found them at this. Don't you teach her anything?"

"Who let her stay after school! Who gives permission for all these things? You are always the one, Aibek. If you left it to me, she would come home every day. She would not have these permissions!"

Mama and Papa continued to shout at each other. They hadn't had an argument this bad since Papa had no work, and the sound of this fighting hammered in Maya's ears and she felt weak and sick. As they blamed each other, they seemed to forget Maya was there and she crept along the wall to the bathroom. Maya slipped in and sat on the cold floor next to the toilet in case she had to be sick. She hugged her knees and sobbed into Soldat's fur while waves of sickness swept over her and her skin prickled with sweat.

Mama and Papa's angry voices rose and fell like the pounding of thunder and then Maya heard a bang, so fierce that the light bulb hanging from the ceiling swayed with its force. Papa slamming the front door. Then she heard the engine of the cab and a sharp squeal as he sped away.

Next came pounding on the bathroom door and a fierce rattling of the handle and Maya wanted to climb out the window with Soldat. He would jump on the toilet seat and leap through the window after her, as graceful as a deer leaping through the forest. They would run like the wind, behind the Mini-Mart, sailing together past the E-Z Day Cleaner, past the bus stop in an easy gallop through the crosswalk. As they ran, each traffic light they came to would turn green until there was a string of green lights glowing like a necklace of emeralds strung all down the street. And then they would be at the Lui's house. Mrs. Lui would greet them in her red Nordstrom coat with the gold buttons. She would hug Maya and hold her close. Then she would bend gracefully like a ballerina and stroke Soldat's soft head, telling him what a good dog he was to bring Maya there safely. Then Mr. Lui would say, "Hi honey," and make the hamburgers. "Want to use the phone, Maya?" Mrs. Lui would say. "Talk as long as you want, we have an extra line for the kids."

"Oh, by the way," Mr. Lui would say, "Shannon is having Kevin and some other kids over Friday night for pizza and videos. It's fine if there's a guy you want to invite, too."

"Maya! Open this door. Do you want more trouble?" Mama rattled the doorknob so hard Maya thought she'd rip it off.

"I'm coming." Maya's voice caught in her throat as she grabbed the toilet and got to her feet. She felt dizzy as she unlocked the door and held her stomach, still afraid she would be sick.

"You have brought shame to your father and on this family." Mama glared at her.

"Mama, it was just kids joking. Guys from the wrestling team pretending some of us were weights."

"I don't know this weights."

"It was nothing, Mama!"

Her hand flew up and Maya fell back as she slapped her face. "Do not tell me nothing when your father saw you!" she screamed.

Maya held her cheek as Mama turned her back, leaving her there grabbing the sink for support. After a few minutes, when she'd finally stopped crying, Maya splashed her face with cold water and went to her room, got in her pajamas and crawled into bed.

Down the hall she could hear the murmur of Mama and Nurzhan's voices and Maya closed her eyes hoping to sleep. She held Soldat close to her and buried her head in his soft fur. Soldat liked to be under the covers very much. But he didn't sleep, because he wanted to stay alert in case she needed him. As Maya held him tightly, she could feel the beating of his brave heart and then she heard footsteps, the bathroom door closing. More footsteps. Then a shadow across her room blocking the light from the Mini-Mart sign as Mama stood in the doorway. She walked toward Maya, who shut her eyes even tighter, trying not to move.

"Here," Mama said quietly, and put a cold cloth against Maya's cheek. Then she turned and was gone.

Horses and Cows

Papa was gone when Maya woke up the next morning. And even though Mama hadn't yet left for work, it was like she was gone, too. She didn't speak to Maya and didn't even look at her, except once when she came in the kitchen. Maya was getting kasha and she stared at her like Maya was a stranger, then turned and left. Not only was Mama not speaking to Maya, but she didn't speak to Nurzhan, either. This never happened before. Even when Nurzhan was punished for the fight with Jerry Hong, Mama still spoke to him. But as Maya was getting dressed in her room, she heard Nurzhan try to talk to Mama. Maya put her ear to the door to listen.

"It's different here, Mama. I'm sure Maya and those guys were playing. Joking, like in a game."

"Quiet, boy! You know nothing of these things!"

Maya was stunned. Mama hardly ever said a harsh word to her precious boy. Then she heard Mama rush by, and then BAM! The door slammed, and the *kamcha* trembled with the force as their mother left without a word of good-bye to either one of them.

Maya came out of her room and she and Nurzhan just looked at each other. Maya didn't feel happy that Nurzhan got yelled at—she felt bad about the whole thing.

"Did you hear?"

Maya nodded.

"She won't listen."

"Thank you for trying, Nurzhan."

"It did no good," he said with sadness. "They don't know about things here, only their own ways. They are like stone."

"Do you think they will still allow me to still be on the team? We have an extra practice today, but I don't know if I should go." As they stood by the door, Maya looked down at Nurzhan, not quite believing she was asking her little brother for his opinion.

"I think so. Mama didn't say not to—"

"She said nothing. She didn't even speak to me."

"If you had to quit the team I think she would have said this."

"Okay, I will go to practice. Do you have your key? You'll get home first."

Nurzhan reached into the neck of his shirt and pulled up the string that held the key.

"Good. We better go now. I just hope you are right, Nurzhan."

Nurzhan and Maya were quiet as they walked to the bus. She missed his chattering like a monkey, but he seemed to feel better when they got to the corner and he saw Jesse. Shannon was coming, too, running toward them just as the bus rounded the corner. She waved to Maya and as she waved back, Maya tried to pretend she was a different person. She tried to pretend she was someone happy.

It wasn't easy to pretend, because Maya dreaded Language Arts class where she and Daniel would be working on their project. Last night he had seen the cab drive up, he had seen her father; he had heard him shout her name with his voice of raging thunder. What must he think? How could she explain it?

On the way to school Maya listened closely to Shannon discuss what she might wear to the skating party. Shannon had so many clothes, she had trouble figuring out what to wear and Maya felt honored when she asked her opinion.

"I'm going to wear jeans. That part's easy, don't you think?"

"Oh yes, I think so."

"You're going to wear jeans, too. Right?"

"Yes." Maya didn't say it, but she wondered if she'd even be going to the party after what happened with Papa.

"I just can't decide if I should wear a dressy sweater,

like my purple one or my red one. Or if I should be more casual, like a sweatshirt," Shannon said, thoughtfully. "Since skating is really a sport, and you can get hot and sweaty."

All the way to school they talked about this, whether the skating party was like doing a sport or going to a party. For Maya it was good to have something else to consider, but as soon as they got to school and went their separate ways, her dread returned. To Maya it was like a toothache that came back after the medicine wore off and Shannon had been the medicine. She just hoped with all her might that Daniel would have forgotten what happened.

But as soon as she got to class and the second Ms. Coe told them to begin work on their projects, Daniel began talking about it.

"Man, your dad is one dude people would not want to mess with."

Maya bit her lip, not knowing what to say.

"What made him go off like that?" Daniel opened the atlas they had been working with. "Wonder if we can go on the net, today?" Then he looked at the back of the room at the computers.

Maya looked at the computers and saw all the same people from yesterday there. "I think we have to sign up."

"Okay, I'll go sign us up."

Daniel left and Maya thought she'd been saved from

talking about her father, but the minute he got back he started in again.

"So what made him go off like that?"

"He only wants me to do schoolwork after school," she said quietly.

"But you're on the team. That's after school."

"The team's okay, but—"

"So when he saw us kidding around he didn't think that was gymnastics or school stuff."

Maya nodded.

"Man, that's strict. Is that how it is where you came from? Kazakhstan?" He smiled. "See I can say it now."

"Guys and girls don't do much together until they're older. And the parents have to know the guy."

"I heard about a country where a father didn't like the guy his daughter married—she had gone ahead without his permission, so he cut her head off and paraded around the town with her head. And it was called an honor killing or something and the father was never arrested. I hope it wasn't Kazakhstan!"

"No, it's not that bad. My Dad wouldn't cut off my head, just my hope."

"What d'ya mean?"

"I've been hoping to go to the skating party, but now I'm not sure if I can go."

"Really?" Daniel looked surprised. "You mean he might not let you go 'cause he saw us fooling around?"

Maya nodded.

Daniel was quiet for a minute. "That's heavy," he said. "Well, let me know as soon as you find out, okay?"

She nodded again. Maya couldn't think of anything else to say, so she opened her notebook and found where they'd left off. She pushed the paper toward Daniel and pointed to the middle of the page. "We're here."

"Oh yeah." Daniel read the paper. Maya thought he must read slowly, even more slowly than she read because it took him a long time. She watched his lips move as he read and Maya began to wonder if Daniel actually had trouble reading. This idea surprised her because she always thought Americans were better at reading and speaking than she was. It was hard for her to believe they could struggle with the English language. And then Maya wondered if it was possible that Daniel wanted her to tell him about Kazakhstan and do the work because he wasn't a good reader and not just because he was lazy.

Finally, Daniel looked up from the paper. "So we were doing the typical family stuff."

"Yes, the daily life."

"Looks like we didn't get to the food."

"No."

"We should have started there." Daniel grinned. "Food. One of my favorite subjects."

Maya laughed at Daniel as he started to name off all his favorite foods. "McDonald's French fries are the best. Next comes Godfather Pizza, then chocolate chip cookie dough ice cream—"

"Are you working on your reports, people?" Ms. Coe looked over at them.

Daniel grabbed his pencil and pulled the notebook to his side of the desk. "So what kind of food? I'll make a list, you just tell me."

"Well, a lot of rice and—"

"Let's go in order, like start with breakfast."

"Okay."

"For breakfast we usually eat kasha."

"What's that?"

"We eat it hot, it is cereal. Stores here have kasha."

"Never heard of it. Okay, what about lunch?"

"Oh *beshbarmak*, and tea."

"*Beshbarmak?*

"It's broth."

"Only liquid?"

"No, it has noodles with meat, onion and then we might have some potatoes—"

"French fries? Yum."

"No, boiled. Most food is boiled. Oh, and sometimes *pilimeny.*"

"What's that?"

"It's like a dumpling. And we have special salad, beets with pomegranates. It's very good. Then for dinner, usually some rice, and some kind of meat like chicken, or lamb or horse or—"

"Horse!"

"Yes. I know people in American don't eat horse, but in Kazakhstan they do."

"Geez. Did you ever eat a horse?"

"Sure. Why is it different than eating a cow?"

"I don't know. I guess it's just what you're used to."

"Not much fish though. Not like here."

"Why's that?"

"It's too far from water. See?" Maya showed him on the map, then Daniel noticed that the computer was free.

"Hey, let's see what kind of stuff there is on the net?"

"Okay." Maya followed him to the back of the room and they took the two chairs in front of the computer. Daniel grabbed the keyboard right away and asked Maya how to spell Kazakhstan again. She told him and watched him type in the letters. It took him so long that Maya began to wonder if the reason he got it mixed up with Afghanistan and Pakistan was because he had problems learning. Maybe he made it seem like a joke to cover up.

119

"Man, there's a lot of stuff." Daniel seemed surprised as long lists of articles and references to Kazakhstan came up on the screen. "I never even heard of this place before."

It made Maya feel good that there were so many articles about Kazakhstan, but they couldn't start to choose which ones to read because Ms. Coe said it was time to put things away and get ready for the bell.

They walked back to their desks and got their books. "Be sure and tell me about the skate. Let me know tomorrow, okay?"

"Okay," Maya nodded, hoping tomorrow Papa would be calm again, like a smooth sea after a storm has passed, and that she'd have good news for Daniel about the party. She knew what she'd wear, too. Maya had been thinking about it ever since the moment Papa signed the permission slip. Even though her choices weren't as complicated as Shannon's, she still enjoyed planning her outfit. She'd wear the pale blue sweater she'd gotten at Costco, and not her Seahawks sweatshirt. Because Maya didn't think the Seventh Grade Skate was a sport. She thought it was a special party.

After gymnastics Maya didn't go outside with the others to wait for the bus. She couldn't take the chance. It was not that she worried that Daniel would pick her up the way he had yesterday, but if there were just a few boys talking to a few girls and Papa came by it could be terrible.

So Maya stayed in the gymnasium and waited next to the gym office so she could look through the window and see when the bus arrived. The gym office had two windows, one that looked into the gym and a window opposite it on the outside wall of the school. Through the windows she saw Shamika and Catherine from her team and Daniel and Steve were there, too. The boys were clowning and the girls were laughing. The window next to the gym had heavy wire covering it so balls wouldn't break it and as Maya looked through the wire, she felt locked away from everyone, like a prisoner behind bars.

Ms. Coe was in the office finishing some paperwork and glanced up and saw her. "Maya, can I help you with anything?"

"No, thank you. I'm just waiting for the bus."

Ms. Coe looked out at the group waiting on the sidewalk. "You don't want to wait outside with your teammates?"

Maya shook her head.

"Is something wrong?"

Maya didn't answer; she didn't know what to say.

"Come on in, you can sit here while you wait."

Maya hesitated a minute then went in the office and sat on the metal folding chair next to the door. It was strange being alone with Ms. Coe. Usually Ms. Coe was in front of the whole class or the whole team. The only time she had seen her alone was the day that Maya stopped in before school when Ms. Coe had asked her to be on the team.

Ms. Coe continued to work on her papers and Maya didn't want to stare at the kids outside so she just looked at the floor. She noticed there was a curving stain in the linoleum that was shaped like a snake.

Ms. Coe put a paper clip on the papers. "How do you like the team? Are you getting along with the girls okay, Maya?"

"Oh yes. I love the team."

Ms. Coe looked out the window where Daniel and Steve were hanging around the girls. "The boys on the wrestling team like our gymnasts." She smiled, watching Daniel try to do a cartwheel. "They seem to be having fun."

"I wish my father thought that," Maya mumbled, surprising herself with the words that had slipped out, half hoping Ms. Coe hadn't heard. Then she looked at the stain in the floor some more.

"Your father?"

Maya looked up. Ms. Coe's face was so kind, and she felt so safe with her that she told Ms. Coe about what happened. It just spilled out. "My father drove by in his cab and saw us joking like that yesterday and ordered me to leave the group he was so angry. Then he blamed my mother and said I was a toy for American boys."

"Oh Maya, I'm so sorry." Ms. Coe sighed.

"I hate being different." What Maya really hated was

that her parents were so different but she didn't say that. It would make her feel bad and she already felt as though she'd betrayed them.

"You know, it's not just parents who have recently come to this county who have a tough time when their children become teenagers. Maya, all parents have a hard time."

"We weren't doing anything, Ms. Coe."

"I know you weren't."

"If you understand this, then why can't parents?"

"Well, they realize that the bodies of some young teens are ready to have children at twelve and thirteen. So sometimes when they see boys and girls flirting they worry that the hormones and their bodies will take over and kids will be tempted to want to mate, tempted to have sex. Biology can be very strong. And that really scares them because boys and girls this young sure aren't ready to be parents." Ms. Coe laughed. "Things are totally out of whack the way humans have evolved."

Maya really didn't know what Ms. Coe was saying, the part about "evolved." It wasn't a spelling word they'd had. So she did what she always did when she didn't understand: she kept quiet.

Ms. Coe just kept explaining. "When people only lived to be about thirty or forty, it worked out all right if people had children so young. But today, people live much longer so childhood lasts much longer. But our bodies are still maturing at twelve and thirteen, actually sometimes earlier with our good nutrition and medicine." Ms. Coe laughed again, "it's kind of a mess. If we could re-design it, we'd probably make sure humans weren't physically ready to have children until their mid-twenties or early thirties."

Maya couldn't believe she and Ms. Coe were having this conversation. She was so surprised at how Ms. Coe was talking to her. They learned about sex in health class, but this was just talking and not really like a teacher up in front of the class teaching while they looked in their books. And Ms. Coe was so easy with her words that Maya wasn't too embarrassed. Maybe a little embarrassed, but not so bad. If only I could talk to Mama like this, she thought.

"I just like this boy, that's all," Maya finally told her. "I only want to skate with him, not more than that."

"Maya, that's like most girls your age, they don't really want to have sex. Not in middle school or even the early years of high school. For the most part they just want to be held, holding hands, or being in a boy's arms—having physical closeness but not actual sex."

"Then I can't believe my father is so angry."

"Probably because boys, even though most of them are quite terrified, are often more curious and eager to have sex and most fathers know this. And since your father is from another culture, it may be even harder for him."

Maya wanted to ask Ms. Coe what to do about her

father, but then she saw the activity bus pull up and she had to go. Maya didn't want to leave. She would have liked to stay with Ms. Coe for a long time.

As the bus left the parking lot, Maya saw through the driver's windshield a cab the color of a lime driving slowly on the street toward the school. Papa had come by to check up on her. She knew this as surely as she knew her own name. Perhaps he'd been driving around the block, looking at the school, watching for her. Maya bit her lip and looked out the window as the cab passed the bus. How many times had he driven by? Had Daniel seen him?

The house was quiet when Maya came in and Nurzhan was sitting at the kitchen table actually doing his work. "Maya," he called from the kitchen when he heard the front door slam. "Could you help me with my spelling?"

"Yes. In a few minutes. I have to do some of my own work first."

Maya didn't really have to do her work; she'd finished it all in class and in the library after lunch. But she went in her room and took her notebook out to write in her journal. Thoughts were whirling in her head and she needed to put them in her journal so they wouldn't give her a headache.

Tuesday

I hate that I do not know if I can go to the skate. It is like

125

I sit on the thin and fragile limb of a tall tree not knowing if it will break, not knowing what will happen to me. At this moment I wish my parents were like American parents, just like Mr. and Mrs. Lui. I was ashamed today when Daniel spoke of my father, wondering if he were like some madman who cut off his daughter's head. I felt shame that we are different. I only want to be like everyone else, not foreign. That is how I feel. Foreign, and not fitting in. But I also feel foreign in my own family. Papa and Mama do not know my world and that makes me foreign from them. If only I had a mother like Ms. Coe. Someone who understood my life. Today when I talked to her I thought I could tell her anything. Even my thoughts of the most embarrassment and she would understand. Even Soldat cannot help me with these things. He is brave and good, but there are things he cannot understand because he is a dog.

To Skate or Not to Skate

The skating party was now two days away. Every day that week, Maya had hoped for some word from her parents about the party—but they hadn't said a thing. *Necho*. On Wednesday night, just two nights before the party, Maya talked to Nurzhan about her problem.

"Nurzhan," she asked, "Mama and Papa have not spoken a word to me about the skating party tomorrow. Do you think I can still go? Do you think the silence is the same as the gymnastics team—that they would tell me if the answer was now 'no'?"

"Maybe the silence means 'yes' or maybe it means 'no.' I don't know."

"Nurzhan, you are no help." Maya snapped at him as if to bite off his little head.

"I'm sorry, Maya." A hurt look covered his face and she felt bad.

"No, I'm sorry I spoke with a sharp voice." Maya apologized and sighed. "It's not your fault."

Their house was silent that night as it had been all

week. Silence itself wasn't unusual in the evenings. Maya's parents would often be so exhausted from work, they'd be too tired to talk. Mama's head would even nod as she tried to study English and Papa's too, while he watched TV. Even though he really liked watching basketball, sometimes in the middle of a game his eyes would close and his head would fall on his chest.

But the quiet this week seemed different than the usual quiet tired times. Even though they lived together in a small apartment and were often in the same room, it was like there was a great distance between everyone. The distance was between Maya and Mama, between Maya and Papa, between Mama and Papa, and even between Mama and Nurzhan. Maya thought it was probably between Papa and Nurzhan, too. She realized it was between everyone except her and Nurzhan. They'd become closer. It was strange, Maya thought, but it seemed like the teams in their family were shifting. She and Nurzhan understood things that their parents weren't able to, and they were learning to count on each other. Also, her brother was a person (not a dog who lived in her mind) and they were beginning to be on the same team.

But Nurzhan didn't know any more than she did what her parents' silence meant. Maya tried to think of what Shannon or Ms. Coe would advise and she knew they'd both give her the same advice. "Maya," they would say, "just ask your parents. Ask them directly if you can still go to the party." They wouldn't understand how difficult it would be for her to follow this advice, but Wednesday night when she was washing dishes and Mama was studying her English book, Maya decided to try.

"Mama?"

No answer.

"Mama?" Maya bit her lip. *Can I go to the skating party?* She heard the words in her mind but they got stuck there and wouldn't come out.

Her mother looked up from her book. She frowned and her dark eyes were hard. Her concentration had been interrupted and Maya knew she was annoyed.

"Nothing…sorry," Maya mumbled.

Mama sighed with irritation, then looked back at her book. As Maya stared at the gray filmy water in the dishpan, she knew she'd never try again. She couldn't risk another explosion ripping apart their home.

All week Maya had been pretending to Daniel that she could probably go to the skate. Like an actor in a play, she acted the part of a cheerful person. Every day Daniel asked her if she was going to the skate, and Maya would smile and say, "Oh probably." At school, she acted the part so well that she almost began to believe that she actually might be going. The day before the skate when Maya was at her locker after her math class, Daniel came up to her.

"Hi-ya, Maya," Daniel leaned on the next locker with his head close to her. The way he said Maya's name and the way his blue eyes crinkled and sparkled made her laugh. "So can you go tomorrow?"

Maya smiled and her heart moved so fast and she felt her borscht face so hot she was afraid he would think she was sick with fever.

"Oh probably," Maya kept smiling.

"Hey, can you skate backwards?"

"No. Not really." Her heart kept pounding.

"Well, I'll teach you." Then put his hand on her shoulder for a minute. "Well, gotta go. See-ya, Maya." Daniel turned and trotted down the hall, weaving between people like he was dribbling with a basketball. At least I'll soon know if I can go to the skate, Maya thought, so much pretending really *is* making me feel sick.

As Maya was bending over to get her health book from the bottom of her locker, out of the corner of her eye she saw a pair of legs heading in her direction. Several people were walking strangely close to the lockers and Maya heard a voice she thought she recognized, although she couldn't place it.

These people got closer and closer. They were bearing down on her like an army tank and Maya started to feel afraid. What were they doing? Why were they coming straight toward her? *Don't they see me?* Maya tried to move out of the way but they were there almost on top of her and a leg lashed out and she felt the pain of a sharp kick! Maya fell over, crashing on the cold floor of the hall and her head banged against the metal base of the locker. Maya lay sprawled on the floor, her backside aching from the force of the kick and she was too scared even to scream.

Nadine Slodky towered over her, glaring down with hate in her eyes.

"Keep your butt outa the middle of the hall, witch," she snarled, then threw back her head and laughed with the girl next to her. Maya struggled to her feet and grabbed her books, knowing she had her borscht face, flaming with anger and humiliation as she heard their laughter cackling all down the hall.

Tears stung her eyes, and Maya wished she'd seen Nadine coming, it would've given her time to have Soldat with her. Carefully, she felt her head where it had banged against the locker and there was a tender bump raised on her scalp. Maya closed her eyes, and could feel Soldat's warm fur against her cheek. Maybe if he'd come earlier he would have given me the courage to stand up to Nadine and fight for myself in some way that wouldn't get me suspended like Nurzhan, she thought. Or maybe he would have jumped against me to warn me so I could get away before I got kicked.

On her way to her next class, Maya hurried along

feeling her head every few minutes and realized she was paying a high price for her relationship with Daniel Moran. The price of Papa's anger and the price of Nadine Slodky's hatred. I should forget this popular boy, she thought. Nothing but trouble has come into my life because of him. Maybe my life wasn't so interesting before I met Daniel Moran, but I wasn't hated and I wasn't causing all this trouble at home. Wouldn't my life be better without this? Maya closed her eyes trying to imagine going back to the days before Daniel. But then she couldn't help remembering his blue eyes when he leaned close to her and said, "Hi-ya, Maya," and she imagined him holding her hands as he taught her to skate backwards, gently lifting her if she started to fall. And she remembered the feel of his shirt against her cheek when he held her like a weight lifter and these thoughts were delicious, sweet thoughts like cotton candy. But it was cotton candy that gave you a stomach ache.

In her Language Arts class, Ms. Coe had a lot of sayings and quotations hanging on the walls. One of Maya's favorites was "Failure is the opportunity to begin again." This always helped her to not be afraid and to keep trying. To keep trying when she failed to say the correct English word. But today Maya thought about this quotation and the skating party. If I failed to go to this party, could I begin again somehow? Would there be another opportunity?" Maya didn't know the answer to this, but she finally decided that since Mama or Papa had not said she couldn't go, that she would be brave and just go ahead and go. She'd have what Ms. Coe calls a positive attitude; she'd believe that everything would be all right.

The night before the party, Maya tried on her jeans and her light blue sweater. Shannon had given her some peach-colored lip gloss and Maya put it on, experimenting with how much to use. She also had some clips and a scrunchy and was trying different hair styles. Her hair came to her shoulders and Maya thought it wasn't interesting. She pulled it back and made a horse-tail with part of it at the back of her head, letting the rest fall to her shoulders. She was surprised at her reflection. She looked different to herself. Older. Maya smiled at the girl in the mirror. Tomorrow she might be at the skate!

As Maya left the bathroom, the front door opened then slammed shut. The living room was dark except for a stream of dim light from the bathroom shining like a faded spotlight where she stood. Papa paused by the door and stared at her. Then he flipped on the living room light and moved toward her. "What's this? What have you done to yourself?" The color rose in his face.

"I'm just trying on my outfit for tomorrow, Papa."

"Tomorrow? What tomorrow?"

"For the skating party."

"Are you crazy, daughter? How could you think this!"

"But you said nothing about me still being on the team. And when you said nothing about the skating party—"

"The team is girls," Papa spat out the words. "The party is boys. You should know this. I should not have to tell you."

"You mean I can't go to the skating party tomorrow?"

"*Nyet*! No party! No boys! I forbid this!"

NADINE STRIKES AGAIN

That night as Maya tried to sleep, Papa's words *Nyet...no party...no boys...Nyet..no party...no boys* echoed through the tunnel of her mind and tears fell between each word.

"Maya?" Nurzhan whispered, "are you all right?"

Maya wiped her face on her pajama sleeve and looked across the bedroom. The Mini-Mart sign blinked on and off through the torn shade and when the orange light flashed on Nurzhan's bed she saw him propped on his elbows looking over at her with a face full of worry.

"I can't go to the party."

"Papa said 'no'?" he asked.

She wiped her face again with her sleeve. It was hard to speak through her tears but she began to breathe in and out with the blinking rhythm of the Mini-Mart sign and after a moment Maya could talk. "He said, 'no party. No boys.'"

"They understand nothing!" Nurzhan sat up. "They are too hard!"

"Shhh, Nurzhan. They'll hear us. Go to sleep."

Nurzhan lay back down and quickly fell asleep while

Maya lay in bed staring through the shade at the blinking sign. She watched the orange light blinking, on and off... on and off...on and off...for what seemed like hours until finally she fell asleep, too.

In the morning Maya waited to get dressed until Mama and Papa had left for work. She didn't want them to see her. She didn't want them to see that she was dressed in her best blue sweater and that she had fixed her hair in the new way and her lips glistened with Shannon's peach lip gloss. Maya got herself ready like this because she'd come up with a plan. All day at school, she'd act like she was going to the Seventh Grade Skate. Then after school, when everyone went to the special bus that would take them to the skating rink, she would get on the regular bus and go home. She'd make up some reason to tell Mr. Foster why she couldn't go as he stood by the bus door checking off names.

As she waited for the bus that morning, she tried to think of a reason to tell Mr. Foster, but her mind was like an empty chalkboard that had been erased. It was strange, she thought, last year when I was in English Language Learner class I didn't have to make things up. But everything is so complicated now in mainstream classes—it seems I need to tell lies just to make my way. Maya didn't like having to make things up, it didn't make her feel good. She'd rather just be able to tell the truth, but there were times when lies seemed the better choice, like when she changed what the principal said to protect Nurzhan. That didn't seem like a bad thing. Maybe the lie she'd tell about why she couldn't go to the skate was the same kind of lie, only to protect me instead of Nurzhan, she thought. To protect me from everyone thinking I was weird. This kind of lie wouldn't hurt anyone, could it be so bad?

On the bus, Maya wanted to tell Shannon the truth that she wasn't going, but she couldn't. Shannon was talking fast, smiling and laughing as she showed Maya a small plastic bag with blue flowers on it where she put some make-up. "I'll have a few minutes to fix my make-up after last period. The girls' bathroom is right next to my computer class."

She unzipped the bag and showed Maya the things she had in it: lipstick, a mirrored compact with powder and a nice little puff, a comb and a small brush, hand cream, a tiny bottle of a perfume sample, and mascara. There were so many things, Maya wondered how she'd have time to put all of them on before she caught the bus. But Shannon had a lot of experience with this sort of thing and Maya was sure she'd been practicing for years. She'd be able to put everything on quickly, without smudging and making a clown face the way Maya was sure she would if she tried to put on all those things.

At school, with her hair fixed in the new way, everyone

thought Maya was going to the skate. In Language Arts when Daniel saw her, he said, "You look different" and she could tell by the way he smiled that he thought it was a nice difference.

"It's just my hair, that's all."

"So, you're going for sure." He said like it was a fact, and a fact that made him happy.

Maya smiled at him and nodded. Underneath her smile her heart was sad. It was as though she was a package with a cheerful wrapping paper on the outside, but inside the package was empty and dark.

She was glad when Language Arts was finally over and she didn't have to be near Daniel anymore with the empty package of her sad heart. The rest of the day she thought of what she would tell Mr. Foster when she didn't board the bus for the skate. It would have to be a reason everyone would believe. At first Maya thought of saying she felt sick, but then they might make her go to the nurse, or they'd call Mama or Papa to come get her. So, she discarded that idea. Next she thought of saying that her brother was sick and she had to go home to take care of him. But their bus stopped at Evergreen first and it was possible someone would see Nurzhan on the bus and they would know he was healthy as a little piglet.

Maya finally decided to tell Mr. Foster that Mama was sick and she had to help her at the doctor. Mr. Foster knew that students like Maya whose parents don't speak English often have to help parents with these things. She was sure he'd believe her.

After the last bell, Maya walked quickly to the special skating party bus. She felt relieved to see that she was one of the first to arrive. Just a few boys were sitting on the bus toward the back, and Maya didn't know them, which made it easier for her. She thought most of the girls would be in the bathroom like Shannon putting on make-up, so if she told Mr. Foster quickly she might be able to leave for the regular bus without anyone she knew seeing her.

Mr. Foster stood by the door to the bus holding a clipboard.

"Hello, Maya," he looked at the clipboard to find her name.

"I cannot go, Mr. Foster. My mother has to go to the doctor and I must go to translate."

"Sorry to hear that," he looked concerned. "Nothing serious I hope?"

"No, I don't think so. But I must go right home. Mr. Foster?

"Yes?"

"Could you tell Shannon Lui what happened? I was supposed to meet her here."

"Sure." Mr. Foster crossed out Maya's name. "Hope your mother's better."

"Thank you." She turned quickly, hoping he wouldn't see her tears, and she ran for the regular bus.

As soon as Maya got home she changed into her ordinary school clothes, took apart her new hair style and wiped off the lip gloss. There was hardly any left, maybe none at all. She thought it had all worn off during the day, but she wiped her mouth anyway.

Maya didn't feel like doing work and just sat on the couch with Nurzhan like a turnip watching cartoons on TV and all the time she was wondering what it was like for all the others at the rink. But she didn't have to wait until Monday at school to find out how it was, because in the middle of a commercial for some new kind of cereal the phone rang. It was Shannon. She'd just gotten home.

"Maya, hi. It's me. Is everything okay?"

"Yes. It's okay."

"Mr. Foster told me. Bummer. Is she okay?"

"Yes. But Shannon, how was the skate?"

"I skated with Kevin almost the whole time—it was incredible! Well, I guess not exactly the whole time. At first he just hung with a bunch of guys, Derrick White, David Pfeiffer, and Norm Schwartz, and they chased each other around and acted like the girls weren't there. You know how they are."

"Oh yes." Another lie. Maya didn't know how they were. She'd never been to a skating party or anything with boys. *No party. No boys.* Maya listened to Shannon talk about everything Kevin said and did after he and the boys stopped chasing each other around.

"Did you see Daniel?" Maya felt timid to ask this, but while she'd been listening to Shannon, Soldat came next to her and she patted his head and found courage.

"Oh Maya," her voice got quiet. "I don't know how to tell you."

"What? Tell me what thing?"

Shannon sighed. "Well, he asked me where you were and I told him what Mr. Foster said."

"Then what happened?"

"Oh, I almost forgot, another guy was next to us when I told Daniel, and this other guy asked me if it was for sure you weren't coming. Some guy. I didn't know him."

"What did he look like?"

"I couldn't really say, he was Asian, one of those kind of invisible people."

Maya wasn't sure what she meant by "invisible" but she thought it meant someone not popular or important. Maya waited for Shannon to tell about Daniel, but she didn't say anything. "Shannon," Maya asked, "what happened with Daniel?"

Shannon sighed again. "Well, he just skated off and the next thing I knew he was with Nadine Slodky. They skated together the whole time. He was all over her and I heard on the bus going home that they're now back together."

Maya bit her lip and thought of Soldat next to her. She patted his soft head and he licked her hand, his tongue was warm and his brown eyes were clear and true. Soldat was with her and helped her not cry.

"He's a jerk, Maya. I'm telling you. The guy's a player and he's not worth your time. You're much too good for him. Listen, I'll see you at school. My sister needs to make a call. Luv ya, Bye."

Click. Maya heard the dial tone and was alone with Soldat. What she wanted right then was to be like Nurzhan. She wanted to be sick with a fake cough so she could stay home from school Monday. She thought, maybe I could cough and cough and Mama would worry about me and put her hand on my cheek and say sweet things to comfort me the way she does with Nurzhan. Maya coughed a few times to try this idea but right away felt foolish. Her cough didn't sound much like a real cough; she thought she sounded like a goat. Even though Maya was an actor at school, she couldn't seem to do a fake cough the way Nurzhan did. She would have to go to school Monday and face Daniel, who was now back together with Nadine. Just to think of having to sit next to him made her feel like a moldy piece of bread that was tossed out from the refrigerator.

But one thing she knew for sure. She would never let

Daniel know she felt like moldy bread. And by the time Monday came around, she'd prepared herself to behave with indifference. She liked the word "indifference." It had been one of their spelling words. Maya decided she'd only talk about the work on their project and act as though Daniel meant no more to her than a small ant crawling along the sidewalk.

"Hi-ya, Maya," Daniel grinned as he walked into class and slipped into the seat next to her. He took out his notebook and pushed it toward her, leaning his head close to her. "Where were you Friday?" he whispered.

"My mother was sick, I couldn't go."

"There's always the next one." Daniel slipped his arm around the back of her chair and smiled again, and Maya's indifference melted like ice on a summer day. Did I misunderstand Shannon? she wondered. Why was he acting like nothing had happened? Maybe he wasn't back together with Nadine, and Shannon had been mistaken. It was hard for her to concentrate on their work with so much confusion in her mind. What did he mean, "there's always the next one?" Did he mean he wanted to go to the next one with her? But how could that be if he and Nadine were going together? Am I so confused because my English isn't good enough?

Maya couldn't wait for the day to end so she could go to the one place where she never felt confused, where it never felt like a strange planet and she never thought about wishing she were back in the English Language Learner class. The gym. She loved it there, and unlike so many things at Beacon, it didn't even look that different from the gymnasium she remembered from Kazakhstan. Her teammates were beginning to feel like special sisters and she loved being with them and she loved the uneven bars, which they were working on that week. Swinging so high in the air, Maya felt free and open and strong. Working out with the gymnastics team had become like a magic cure to help ease whatever difficult thing happened each day at school.

After the last bell, she put her books in her locker and headed for practice. The door to the gym was next to the door that goes outside to where the buses park. As soon as school got out, there was always a big jam and it seemed to her like the whole school crowded into that one hallway.

Maya was inching her way next to the wall heading toward the gym, going the opposite way from the huge crowd in the hall, when someone yelled at her. "Hey what's-your-name. May-ah!"

Maya looked across the sea of bodies and saw Nadine Slodky at the edge of the crowd.

"Hey horse eater! Do you like catsup with Black Beauty?" Nadine yelled.

Every head in the whole hall turned to stare at her.

"Don't let that girl near a race track!" Nadine yelled again and then laughed. "They eat horses where she comes from."

The girls with Nadine cracked up and a girl in a Mariners sweatshirt pointed at her. Their laughter and horse jokes continued as Maya fought her way through the crowd, desperately trying to get to the gym.

Maya's stomach ached like the time Nadine kicked her and her borscht face was burning. She called Soldat and he was waiting for her in the gym and he walked with her to the locker room. As Maya put her arms around his neck and buried her face in his soft fur, it seemed to her that so many times since she'd left the English Language Learner class to be in this mainstream, she had been drowning in it and the mainstream was an icy river full of danger. In her mind she told Soldat what she now understood to be true. I am a joke to Daniel and Nadine and everyone they know. His interest in me was only to make a joke of me and just as I'd thought in the beginning, he only wanted to get me to do all the work on our report. Then he used the things I told him about our family's life in Kazakhstan to make me the joke of the school. All Maya wanted to do was go home and crawl under the covers of her bed and never come back.

But as she started to go, Maya looked out into the gym through the locker room and saw her teammates. They were blurry because of her tears, but as she saw them stretching and warming up she knew she couldn't leave. She couldn't let them down. Or Ms. Coe. Maya remembered what she and Ms. Buckman had said, "There's nothing more important than giving each other support and encouragement. We ask courage of ourselves and we must en-courage each other." So Soldat stayed by Maya's side while she splashed cold water on her face and then as she changed into her leotard.

She couldn't remember ever needing her dog so much. He stayed with her throughout practice, too. He vaulted with her, he sat on the end of the beam, he danced on his legs while she did her floor exercise routine, and he waited faithfully at the bottom of the bars while she sailed through the air.

While Maya was on the bars she wanted to sail higher and higher up through the school into the clouds to a beautiful meadow filled with flowers. There by a clear pool near a stream, she would look at her reflection in the water and she would put on some peach lip gloss and together she and Soldat would run with joy through those flowers in the meadow.

All during practice the team members encouraged each other and when Maya's teammates cheered for her, "Way to go, Maya!...Good try!...You'll get the next one!... Beautiful!...That was fantastic, Maya!" their voices eased the sting of the horse jokes like a soothing salve.

When practice was over, Maya went to the gym office where she looked through the window and waited for the bus. She'd never again take the chance of waiting with everyone else in case Papa drove by.

But today, it wasn't only the fear of seeing Papa that kept Maya inside, it was the fear of seeing Daniel. She couldn't bear the thought of it. Maybe Daniel made jokes and acted silly sometimes because he wasn't good at school, Maya could understand that. Especially since Shannon had said Daniel had an older brother who was such a star at everything. But she couldn't accept that he made jokes that hurt people. And the same thing about Nadine. Maybe she did have a bad life at home, with her father being laid up, like Shannon said. But it still wasn't okay to be mean. Maybe she could understand why someone's mean, but it's still not okay, and she didn't want any part of this anymore.

"Ms. Coe?"

"Good practice, Maya."

"Thanks." Maya went in the office and sat where she always sat to watch for the bus.

"Ms. Coe?"

"Hmmm?" Ms. Coe leafed through a stack of papers, checking them with a red pencil.

"I want to go back to Ms. Chan's English learners class."

Ms. Coe looked up and put down her pencil. Her face was kind and her blue eyes were so true and good that even though Soldat was still by Maya's side, she began to weep. Tears streamed down her face, and then worse than that, sobs began to shake her body as all the humiliation she had carried since Nadine yelled at her was unleashed.

Ms. Coe came around the desk and sat next to Maya. She put an arm around her shoulders, but she didn't say anything. She didn't tell Maya not to cry or ask her what was wrong. She just stayed with her and was quiet. She handed Maya a tissue and after a while when she could talk, Maya told her everything.

"What I don't understand, is why this joke? Here people eat cows. What is so different?"

"And in some cultures it's terrible to eat cows, like in India," Ms. Coe said.

"In Kazakhstan most Kazakh people don't eat pigs."

"Yes, many Muslim people don't eat pork," Ms. Coe said. "I guess it comes down to the fact that people have trouble accepting other people's customs or behavior if it's different from the way they do things."

"I don't understand why it is that there are so many different people here but then it seems like everybody is supposed to act the same. To me that makes it hard here. It was hard also in Kazakhstan and that's why we came, but it was hard in a different way. Everything was like the wreck from a big storm after our country broke away from the Soviet Union. My parents' pay was cut, and everyone's pay and the *tenge,* our money, was worth less and less. And Mama and Papa lost their teaching jobs because the government was running out of money and Mama had to go to the market and sell many of our things—clothes, dishes, even some furniture—and then my grandmother died and everything fell apart and Aunt Madina who was here sponsored us to come and so we left, and then she moved away because of her husband's job." Maya had never told anyone about why they came from Kazakhstan. It seemed to her that no one wanted to know, but Ms. Coe was different and Maya's words flew out like water and steam from the geyser she had seen in a film about Yellowstone Park.

"They made me feel ashamed, Ms. Coe, and I just want to go back to Ms. Chan's."

"It'd be easier there, but your test scores in English are too high now, Maya." Ms. Coe went to her desk. "Let me tell you something Eleanor Roosevelt said. You remember who she was?"

"Her husband was a president."

"Right, and she did many good things for people on her own, too." Ms. Coe got a slip of paper. "I'm going to write this down and I want you to take it home and think about what it means. And we can talk more about it after the next practice."

Maya watched Ms. Coe write on the paper with her blue felt pen, wondering how words from someone such a long time ago could help her with Nadine Slodky. But she didn't speak this thought to Ms. Coe because Maya knew Ms. Coe was trying to help her. Then Ms. Coe handed Maya the paper and she read it. It said:

No one can make you feel inferior without your permission.

Eleanor Roosevelt

Maya looked up and saw the bus pulling up and she carefully put the paper in her notebook. She thanked Ms. Coe and left for her bus. Maya clutched her notebook close to her and thought, now Soldat and I have someone else with us when we get on the bus. Eleanor Roosevelt.

THE LIE COMES TRUE

Maya couldn't believe her eyes when she got to the bus stop because Shannon was there first. Maya couldn't remember another time that had happened and when she saw her standing in the rain with her parka hood pulled down over her forehead, Maya wondered if something was wrong.

"Shannon, you're here early." Maya smiled, hoping she was okay.

"Yeah." Shannon looked away.

"Is everything all right?"

"No. My mom has gone nuts."

Maya didn't say anything. Then the bus pulled up and she followed Shannon to the back. Shannon looked out the window and didn't say anything either, for a while. So Maya just looked out the window, too.

Then Shannon turned to Maya. "This happens every time my grandmother comes to visit. I always think it'll get better, but it doesn't. The week before *Po-po* gets here

Mom starts yelling at us and telling us that we're not Chinese enough."

"What does she mean?"

"Beats me. She just goes nuts. It's my dad's mom and she visits us from California a few times a year and everything at home just falls apart. None of us can do anything right. Mom acts like we're all losers. Big failures and that she's ashamed of us. The way we eat, the way we talk, the way we dress—it's all wrong. Then she makes us drop our lives and clean the whole house like there's going to be a military inspection or something. We can't talk on the phone, we can't go anywhere, it's ridiculous."

"Is your grandmother strict?"

"No, that's what's so crazy. It's my mom's problem. *Po-po* adores us. I mean, I know she's hard on Mom, but never on us. It's just weird."

"What does your Dad do?"

"He just reads the paper and then goes and plays tennis at the indoor courts. I think Mom drives him nuts, too."

Maya was so surprised to hear that things weren't perfect in Shannon's family that she didn't know what to say. It was hard to imagine that Mrs. Lui who wore that red Nordstrom coat with the gold buttons could be going nuts. And that Mr. Lui would escape to the tennis courts.

Shannon and Maya both sat there and just looked out the window. Maya watched the rain as the drops slashed across the glass and felt that her mood matched the dark day. She dreaded school. The last place she wanted to be was on that bus. Finally, when the bus turned the corner and drove down the block toward the school, Shannon said, "I'm sorry to be in such a foul mood. How're things with you?"

At first Maya wanted to just say "oh fine," but instead she told Shannon what happened and how Nadine Slodky had made such a mean joke. She hadn't planned to tell her, but as they got close to school she just blurted it out.

"It just shows how jealous she is of you, Maya."

"Jealous?"

"Sure. After all, Daniel asked you to the skate first, and just got back with her when you didn't show up. I'll bet he's still flirting with you, isn't he?"

"Maybe, I don't know. I'm so confused. I thought you said he was a player and I should just forget him."

"Well sure, but it's not that easy to just forget someone. Especially a guy who's so cute and popular. Don't worry. He'll probably ask you to the seventh grade dance and then dump her."

"I wouldn't go."

"Wouldn't or couldn't?"

"Well, probably I can't go. Papa and Mama don't want me to go to many things after school. They think gymnastics is enough. But even if I could, I wouldn't go with Daniel."

"I thought you were crazy about him?" Shannon looked surprised.

"He is handsome, but he has a mean heart."

"Because of what he told Nadine about eating horses?"

"Yes."

"Boys do dumb stuff like that. He was probably just joking around, and thought it was funny."

"It wasn't funny to me."

During her study period that morning Maya looked on the computer and found a picture of Eleanor Roosevelt. Maya thought Eleanor Roosevelt looked like a very strong person and she closed her eyes and memorized her face and her dress and the nice hat she was wearing. Then when she went to Language Arts, both Eleanor Roosevelt and Soldat came in the class with her. Soldat sat on the floor next to her desk and Eleanor Roosevelt stood right behind Maya in her blue dress and put her hand on Maya's shoulder. When Daniel came to class Mrs. Roosevelt whispered in Maya's ear, "No one can make you feel inferior without your permission."

I don't give Daniel Moran permission, Maya told Mrs. Roosevelt, who gave her shoulder a little pat. Soldat was happy about this, too, and he wagged his tail.

"Hi, Daniel," Maya smiled at him, holding her head high like a strong person who isn't bothered by a dumb boy.

"Hi-ya Maya," Daniel flopped into the seat next to her. "Did ya see the Sonics last night? It was a great game."

"No, I was out," Maya blinked her eyes for a minute and patted Soldat, "with my friends." I certainly was, she thought. I was out with my friends Soldat and Eleanor Roosevelt.

"Anyone I know?"

"No." Maya smiled at Daniel like she had a wonderful secret and he would be devastated (devastated was another one of their spelling words) if he knew it. "Let's do our work," she said in a strong voice, and Eleanor Roosevelt gave her another nice little pat on her shoulder.

Mrs. Roosevelt and Soldat stayed with Maya the entire period and when the bell rang and class was over and Maya looked at Daniel gathering his books, she was shocked at the sight of him. He had changed. Daniel Moran, this most handsome boy, wasn't so good looking. Maya didn't know exactly how it happened because everything about him was the same. He had the same hair, the same face, the same body, the same clothes, but somehow he didn't look so handsome anymore. Maya remembered this happening with Ruby Komar in her English Language Learners class last year, only the opposite. When Maya first saw Ruby she thought she was an okay looking person but not really special looking. Then Maya got to know her and Ruby became beautiful.

Maya didn't feel like she needed Mrs. Roosevelt and Soldat the rest of the day so she told them to go about their business because she'd be okay. And she did feel okay, although on her way to her health class Maya passed Ms. Chan's room and she still wished she could be there. Maybe I'll always wish I could be back where it was safe, she thought.

Outside her health class a girl stood at her locker talking with some other girls. It was the one in the Mariners sweatshirt who had pointed and laughed at her yesterday and Maya's heart pounded with fear at the sight of her.

"Hey, there's that girl Nadine knows, the horse-eater!" She threw back her head and laughed and everyone looked at Maya as she scurried into class like a small mouse terrified at the sight of a fierce cat.

Maya wished she hadn't told Mrs. Roosevelt and Soldat to go about their business, she needed them now and she closed her eyes hoping to feel them near her.

"Maya?"

She opened her eyes and looked up as Tyler Lee took his seat next to her. "I heard that girl—"

"Everyone thinks I'm a joke," Maya whispered. "It's

all because someone learned that in the country we came from people eat horses."

"So what. Some people in my family eat chicken feet."

"Just the feet?"

"No, the whole chicken, too. But my parents and especially my grandmother think the foot of the chicken with the claws and everything is very special."

"In China, they like the feet?"

"Yeah, and one time my grandmother put a chicken foot in my lunch for a special treat for me. I don't like them all that much, but she was trying to be nice. I was sitting with these guys and they saw it and went nuts. One guy grabbed it and threw it around and it was a big joke."

"How long did they joke about this?"

"They called me chicken toe or something for a while but then it stopped and people forgot."

"Do you think they'll forget this horse joke?"

"They will. Just don't let them know it bothers you."

"Thank you, Tyler." Maya smiled at him and he smiled only a small smile then quickly looked at the floor and she noticed that his ears had turned very red. This was the most they'd ever talked and Tyler immediately got quiet and didn't seem to want to say anymore. But Maya was grateful he'd been able to tell her about the chicken foot, and she felt better by the time class was over and looked forward to gymnastics practice.

When Maya got to the gym, Ms. Coe came over to her, walking quickly and carrying a pink slip from a message pad. "Maya, the office just phoned down to the gym trying to find you. They need you to come up and talk to Mr. Haight."

"Did they say why I must do this?" Oh no. Not Nurzhan again, Maya thought.

"No, just that you must go as soon as you can."

"It must be about Nurzhan."

"Nurzhan?"

"My little brother. He gets in fights at his school, then they call Papa or Mama and I have to go there to translate." Maya sighed.

"You better run along, honey. Sorry you have to miss practice."

"I am too!"

All the way from the gym to the office Maya was furious with Nurzhan. Why couldn't he stay out of trouble? Why did he have to ruin things for me? Why can't he get someone like Mrs. Roosevelt in his brain to help him so he doesn't get into these fights when people tease him? That brother is such a stupid boy!

She went to the office and waited in front of the wide counter. Behind the counter were three desks where the school secretaries work and a student receptionist who greets people who come in the office. Maya had only waited a minute when the student receptionist walked over to the counter and asked Maya if she could help her.

"Ms. Coe said I was supposed to come to the office." Maya handed her the pink slip.

As the girl looked at the slip, Mr. Haight came in from his office. "It's Maya, isn't it?"

"Yes."

"Come on back." He motioned for Maya to follow him so she went behind the counter and around the corner to his office.

He closed the door behind them. "We got a call from Mrs. Collins."

Mrs. Collins, what does that have to do with me? Maya wondered, biting her lip.

"She said your mother works for her and there's been an accident," he explained. "I'm sorry, Maya. But she said to tell you…"

Maya didn't hear any more of what Mr. Haight said. The fear that swept over her was so great not even Soldat or Mrs. Roosevelt could help her. She went numb as she tried to understand what Mr. Haight was telling her.

"Mrs. Collins has taken your mother to Harborview Hospital, but she doesn't know how to reach your father. Your mother said for you to come to the hospital. We've called a cab and Mrs. Collins will pay the driver when you arrive at the emergency entrance. It should be here any minute now," he paused. "I'm sorry to have to tell you all this—are you okay?"

Maya nodded, biting her lip.

"Mrs. Collins wanted me to be sure and say that what happened to your mother isn't life threatening." Maya stared at him, her eyes filling with tears, so he explained, "The accident isn't a threat to her life—her life isn't in danger."

The time between when Maya left school and got to the hospital blurred by in a rush of panic and confusion. To her, it was like when Shannon put a video on fast forward and everything rushed by, only this was more than a scary movie on fast forward. It was a nightmare, a frightening dream, that Maya didn't want to believe was really happening.

As soon as the cab arrived at the hospital, a woman in a tan pants suit with a beautiful cream and brown print scarf came out. Her clothes looked like Mrs. Lui's although she had silvery blonde hair.

"Maya dear, I'm Janet Collins. I think your mother has just sprained her ankle, but of course it'll have to be X-rayed to make sure." Mrs. Collins paid the driver and Maya followed her into the emergency room.

Mama sat in a turquoise plastic chair at the end of a row of people all sitting in similar chairs. Her shoe was off and her ankle was huge; it looked like her foot was attached to a very large squash. She lifted her hand in a little wave when she saw Maya, but she didn't smile.

"I want to make sure you've talked to your father and that he'll come before I go ahead and leave," Mrs. Collins said. "Your mother didn't want me to call him until you got here."

Maya translated what Mrs. Collins had said and Mama told her she didn't want Papa to have to come and sit for many hours and lose money. He should go home at the usual time and stay with Nurzhan.

"She would like him to come when it is time for us to go home," Maya told Mrs. Collins.

"Tell your mother that I can't leave until I know for certain you've located him."

"Mama," Maya said in Russian, "she doesn't want to go until she knows for sure we have talked to Papa and he can come here when we are ready to go home."

Mama nodded. "Call Papa and tell him you will stay with me—then call Nurzhan."

Mrs. Collins saw Mama nod and she opened her purse and handed Maya a phone. It was black and shaped like a brick with an antenna rising from the top that looked like a black straw. Maya hadn't seen a phone like it before. "Go ahead and use this, dear."

Mrs. Collins showed her how to dial and Maya called Northwest Cab and the dispatcher put her through to

Papa. Papa sounded very worried and he wanted to come to the hospital right away. Maya didn't want to argue with him so she gave the phone to Mama, who told him to go home after work and stay with Nurzhan. She told him not to come to the hospital until she was ready to go home. Her voice was very firm. Then she handed the phone back to Maya.

"You call me when she's done," Papa insisted.

Yes, Papa." Then he hung up and Maya asked Mrs. Collins if she could call her brother.

"That's fine, dear." Mrs. Collins patted Maya's arm.

When Maya got him on the phone, Nurzhan seemed very scared, so again she gave the phone to Mama. Her mother told him that Papa would be home at the usual time and she said to be a good boy and do his schoolwork. Her voice was very firm, but softer than it had been when she spoke with Papa; and she told him it would be okay. "*Eto normal'no, Nurzhan,*" she said. Then she handed the phone back to Mrs. Collins.

Mrs. Collins put the phone back in her purse and stood up. "I'll find out where there's a phone so you can call your father when your mother's done," she said, and went over to the front desk.

Maya and her mother were quiet while they waited for Mrs. Collins to come back. Mama's ankle seemed to get bigger in front of Maya's eyes. Now it looked like a giant pumpkin and Maya worried that maybe it was broken.

After a few minutes, Mrs. Collins came back. "The people at the information desk in the lobby will let you use the phone," she pointed to a big door at the end of the room. "It's right through there." Then she turned to Mama. "Gulnara, I'm so sorry this has happened. Please have Maya call as soon as you get home to let me know how you are."

Maya translated for Mama and Mama nodded and said, "Thank you," in English.

"Be sure and call me, Maya," Mrs. Collins reminded Maya as she left.

Maya and her mother sat in the emergency room for almost two hours before a nurse called out, "Gulnara Ala-zova." By then the day was gone. Outside the sky was the filmy blue of dusk.

Maya helped Mama from the chair and she put her arm around Maya's shoulder as she tried to walk. The nurse saw Maya holding Mama while she tried to hop on one foot and quickly told them to stay where they were while they got a wheelchair. A few minutes later a guy who Maya thought looked a lot like Roberto Sanchez in her math class—only a little older—came in pushing the wheel-chair. He helped Mama into the chair. He was very gentle and kind and then he wheeled Mama into an examining room. where the nurse was putting a paper sheet over the examining table. The nurse and the guy who looked like Roberto helped Mama out of the chair and lifted her onto the table. Then the nurse looked at Mama's ankle. "How did you injure yourself?" she asked.

"My mother doesn't speak much English so I'll translate," Maya said. Then she told Mama what the nurse had asked and translated Mama's answer. "She'd been on a step-ladder cleaning the top of some windows," Maya said, "when she leaned over too far and lost her balance. Her leg twisted underneath her and she fell on the outside of her foot."

The nurse wrote things on a chart and then took Mama's blood pressure. "The doctor will be in soon to examine you and then you'll have an X-ray."

Maya translated and then they were left alone in the room. Mama closed her eyes and her hands tightly gripped the sides of the steel table. Looking at her mother's pale face, Maya was certain her mother's pain and this misfortune were her own punishment for telling the lie at school. For telling them that she couldn't go to the Seventh Grade Skate because Mama had to go to the doctor and needed her. My lie has come true and it's my fault, Maya thought with a heavy heart. I feel as low as an ugly worm that crawls in the dirt.

It seemed like Maya and her mother waited forever. Maya could hear everything the people said in the next examining room because there was only a green curtain between them. The emergency room was overflowing with people. All the rooms were filled with patients with just green curtains separating people. The voices on the other side of the curtain were angry, a man's voice and a woman's, and she said the accident had been his fault because he wasn't paying attention and he yelled that it was rainy and he couldn't see and why didn't she just shut up. Maya thought it was like listening to voices on the radio since you couldn't see the faces.

Finally, there was a knock on the door, then it opened and another woman came in. She was a very pretty African American woman and Maya thought she looked like someone in a magazine.

"Mrs. Ala-zov-a?" she stumbled over their name.

"Alazova." Maya pronounced it for her as Mama said, "Hello."

"And you're her daughter?"

"I'm Maya. I can translate."

"Good. I'm Dr. Bray. What is your native language?" she asked Mama. Maya translated and then told her what Mama said, that she spoke Kazakh and Russian and that their family had come from Almaty, Kazakhstan.

"When I was in high school we had an exchange program with Seattle's sister city Tashkent in Turkistan, and

I was in the program. I was told Turkistan is quite similar to Kazakhstan."

This reminded Maya of her first conversation with Daniel when he said his cousin had been in a program like that and for a minute before she translated, she felt sad. But then when her mother heard the translation, she smiled at the doctor. Seeing Mama smile made Maya smile, too. It was so unusual for them to meet someone who had been near Kazakhstan, and unusual for Maya to see Mama smile at a stranger, especially when she knew Mama was in so much pain.

Dr. Bray examined Mama's ankle and asked a lot of questions such as, "Which way did you fall? Which way did your ankle turn? Can you put any weight on it? Can you walk at all? Can you bend your ankle?" Then she pressed on Mama's ankle in different places and asked each time, "Does this hurt?" After that she turned Mama's ankle several ways and asked each time, "Does this hurt?"

Maya translated each question and answer exactly as they spoke, then it was time for Mama to go to X-ray. The same guy who looked like Roberto came back and he and the nurse lifted Mama from the table into the wheelchair. Maya followed him as he wheeled Mama down a long hall and through the waiting room. Out the window, the streetlights had come on and car headlights streamed slowly through the darkness. It was night and they still weren't done.

Outside the X-ray room they waited a long time for their turn. There were three people ahead of them, an old man with a red face who kept coughing, a little girl with her parents speaking a language Maya didn't know, and a guy with blond hair who was big and looked like he might play basketball or football. Finally they called Mama's name.

Maya went with Mama and told the X-ray man that she would translate. He explained that Mama would have a lead apron put over her body except for her ankle to protect her from the machine. Mama seemed confused and a look of fear rose in her eyes. Maya told her it was all right and it wouldn't hurt.

"Are you sure?"

"Yes, Mama. It will be okay."

When the X-ray was done a different guy came back with a wheelchair, not the one who looked like Roberto. This man was older and bald. He helped Mama into the wheelchair and then took her back to the waiting room. The clock on the wall over the front desk said eight o'clock. Would they even get home by midnight? The waiting room was even more crowded now, and Maya could hear the sirens of ambulances coming toward the hospital.

It was almost nine o'clock when a different nurse called Mama's name. This nurse was a man. He didn't look that old and his hair was tied back in a ponytail. To Maya, he didn't look like her idea of how a nurse should look. But he was calm and friendly as he wheeled Mama to another examining room where they waited some more. This time there were different people on the other side of the green curtain, but they were whispering and Maya couldn't hear what they were saying. Then, finally, after almost a half hour, Dr. Bray came back.

"We have good news. It's not broken." She smiled. "But it's a severe sprain. We're going to put it in a special splint and you must stay off your feet for two weeks." Dr. Bray handed Maya a prescription. "This is for her pain. She can take one every four hours, and she should be seen again in two weeks, unless the swelling doesn't go down and it seems worse, in that case she should come back. Be sure and have her keep the leg elevated as much as possible."

"Elevated?" Maya didn't know that word.

"Have her keep her leg up, on a footstool or a chair. Or up on a pillow when she's in bed."

Maya translated for Mama and they both thanked Dr. Bray. Then the man with the ponytail came and pushed Mama back to the waiting room and Maya left her there while she went to call Papa. The clock over the front desk said five minutes after ten.

"How is she?" Papa's voice was tense and filled with worry.

"Her ankle isn't broken, Papa."

"Good," he said with a deep sigh.

"But she can't walk."

"I'll be there in ten minutes."

Maya hung up and went back to the waiting room. Mama looked so small and sad in the wheelchair in the room packed with strangers—all of them sick or hurt—that once again Maya felt like an ugly worm whose lie had come true.

Maya's Favorite Chaperone

It was decided that Maya would take Mama's jobs for her while she couldn't work. She wouldn't go to gymnastics practice, instead, right after school she'd go straight to the houses Mama cleaned. The people Mama worked for agreed to this and Maya worked at each house from three-thirty until six-thirty when Papa came to pick her up. She wasn't able to clean their entire houses in this amount of time, but they told her which rooms were the most important and she was able to clean those. Bathrooms were on the list in every house.

Telling Ms. Coe about this was very hard. Maya was afraid she might not want her on the team since she had to miss practice for two weeks. She was afraid she'd find someone else to take her place.

"Maya," she said, "don't worry about the team. Just come back to practice whenever you can."

It helped so much to hear that she'd still have a place on the team. What good news! And it made her want to work very hard at Mama's houses so that she'd also still have her place at those jobs.

Maya didn't mind doing Mama's jobs. Although she did get very tired, and she was scared sometimes that she might break something when she dusted—especially at Mrs. Hathaway's house because she had a lot of glass vases and some small glass birds. But Maya didn't mind vacuuming, mopping, dusting, cleaning cupboards, counters, stoves, and refrigerators. She didn't even mind cleaning toilets. It was as if all the work she did cleaning houses was to make up for the lie she'd told, to make it right. And besides, her family needed the money.

When Maya finished working, as soon as she got home she had to make dinner for everyone. Each day she got more tired and on Wednesday when she was peeling potatoes she cut her finger. Maya thought it was just a little cut so she washed it off and continued to peel.

Nurzhan looked up from the table where he was doing his work. "What's wrong with the potatoes?"

"Nothing," Maya said automatically, with her eyes half-closed.

"They're red!"

"What?"

"The potatoes, Maya. They look like you painted them with red streaks."

Maya looked down and saw her finger bleeding on the

potato and it scared her to be so tired that she hadn't seen this. "It's just blood, Nurzhan. I cut myself. It'll wash off."

"Oh yuk."

"Quiet boy! I said I would wash it off."

That night at dinner Nurzhan refused to eat the potatoes even though there was no sign of blood on them and Maya wanted to take the whole dish and dump them on his head.

The next week she was so tired after going to school and cleaning Mrs. Hathaway's house that she burned the chicken. After Maya put it in the oven, she sat at the table with Nurzhan to do her homework. She put her head down on her book and rested for just a minute and the next thing she knew Nurzhan was pounding on her arm.

"Maya! The oven!" he shouted.

"Oh no!" Smoke was seeping from the oven and Maya leaped up and grabbed a dish towel and pulled the pan from the oven. The chicken was very dark but not black, although all the juice at the bottom of the pan had burned and was smoking. "It's okay, Nurzhan, we can still eat it."

"Good." Nurzhan smiled.

Nurzhan didn't mind the almost burned chicken that night, but Papa did.

"This tastes like my shoe!" Papa grumbled.

"Aibek, Maya is doing the best she can. It is not easy.

She must go to school, then do my work, then cook for us. She is just a young girl."

Maya looked at Mama and felt tears in her eyes. She couldn't remember another time when Mama spoke on her behalf and her tears were the kind you have when you know someone is on your side.

Papa grunted and didn't finish his chicken, but he said nothing more while Mama sat at the table with her leg up on a chair and ate every bite of hers. Maya didn't know if her mother really liked the chicken, but she ate it all.

The two weeks that Maya worked cleaning houses for Mama seemed like two years. When Mama went back to the doctor she got a new kind of splint and the doctor told her she could now go back to work as long as she still put her foot up at night. Mama was happy about this because she hadn't liked sitting home alone with her foot up all day. And Maya was happy because she could go back to gymnastics practice again.

On Monday morning Maya touched the *kamcha* on the way out the door, hoping it would be a good day. She was eager to get back to her normal life. But in homeroom when Mr. Horswill announced there would be an all-school dance a week from Friday and handed out the permission slips, Maya realized things were different. A month ago thinking of the dance would have made her excited, but not now.

Maya looked at the slip and started to crumple it up. What was the use of even taking such a thing home to Mama and Papa? *Nyet…no party…no boys.* Why would I be so foolish to think they would sign?

But then Maya stopped crumpling the permission slip and instead tried to smooth it out. Maybe something had changed. Maybe Papa had a passenger in his cab, an important man whom Papa would respect and the important man would say, "In America in middle school, it is a fine thing for boys and girls to go to skating parties and dances."

And Papa would look in the cab mirror at the important man sitting in the back seat and say, "Yes, I see now that it is a fine thing and I have been wrong about this."

Maya knew that there was probably only one chance in one zillion that Papa would change his mind, but she kept smoothing out the crumpled permission slip anyway and put it in her notebook. She didn't know why she didn't throw it away. Maybe I just can't give up hope, she thought. It's like that in America, it's a place where things can change for people, and so many people always have hope. At least that's how it seemed to her. Maybe she was beginning to think this way too, although her hope was very small.

Coming home on the bus that day, Shannon talked about the dance the whole time. Her grandmother had gone back to California and things were happy again at her house. Their conversation was exactly like the conversations they had before the skating party: planning what clothes they'd wear, how they'd style their hair and wondering what boys would be there and if they'd dance with them. Shannon and her sister had taught Maya how to dance when she was over at their house, and she often practiced alone in the bedroom when Nurzhan was watching TV. She loved to dance.

Shannon and Maya wondered if the boys would ever slow dance or only fast dance and it was so enjoyable talking about this that she almost forgot that she'd never get permission to go.

That evening as dinner was cooking, Maya sat with Nurzhan at the kitchen table and helped him with his spelling words. While she waited for him to think how to spell "admire," she took the permission slip from her notebook and stared at it.

"A…d…m…i…e…r."

"Almost, Nurzhan. It's this," Maya said, as she wrote the correct spelling on the top of the permission slip and turned it for him to see.

"A…d…m…i…r…e," he spelled, then he looked closely at the slip. "What's this for?"

"It's a permission slip for the all-school dance, but it is only good for scratch paper to help you with spelling. Papa will never let me go. I don't know why I trouble myself to keep such a thing."

Nurzhan took the slip and put it in his notebook.

"What are you doing with it?"

"Let me try."

"Try what?"

"Let me try to get permission for you from Papa."

Maya laughed. "Oh, Nurzhan. Don't be foolish. You waste your time. Papa will never change his thinking because of you."

"I will try anyway. When he comes home tonight I will speak to him myself. I have a plan."

Maya could only smile a sad smile at the idea of little Nurzhan trying to change the mind of Papa, who is a man like a boulder.

After dinner Maya went to her room to study, leaving Nurzhan to talk with Mama and Papa. She was afraid to really hope that any good thing could come from Nurzhan's plan. To hope and then be disappointed seemed to be worse. Maya thought it was better to live her dreams through Shannon. She could at least hear every little detail of Shannon's experience at the dance and be happy for her, giving up the idea that she'd ever be the one who goes to the dance, too.

But Maya comforted herself thinking about the dream in her life that really had come true. The gymnastics team.

It was a fine, good thing in her life. Her teammates were her friends and sometimes Ms. Coe seemed like her auntie. The team was a place where she belonged and each day at practice Maya felt like she was with her school family. Maya was feeling content with these thoughts when Nurzhan burst into the room.

"Maya! You can go!" Nurzhan jumped up and down like a little monkey and Maya stared at him in disbelief.

"Don't joke with me about such a thing, Nurzhan!" she snapped.

"No! It's true. Look!" He waved the permission slip in front of her face.

Maya stared at the slip, still in disbelief. *Aibek Alazova...* Papa's name and Papa's writing. *It was true!* She was still staring at the slip, still afraid to completely believe that such a thing could be true, when Mama and Papa came in.

"We give permission for this, Maya, because Nurzhan will go, too," Mama said with a smile. Maya was surprised; her mother's look seemed soft as if she were remembering something pleasant and sweet.

"He has promised he will not leave your side," Papa announced in a most serious tone. "He is your *soprovozhdat'.*"

"Chaperone." Maya said the English word. She knew this word because it was what the parents who help the teachers supervise the kids at school were called. But she hadn't heard of a little boy being a chaperone.

"Thank you, Mama. Thank you, Papa."

"It is Nurzhan you must thank," Mama said, smiling again her soft smile.

Maya thanked Nurzhan, too and Mama and Papa left their room. Then she heard the front door close and knew Papa had left for work.

That night Nurzhan and Maya whispered in their beds after Mama had gone to bed.

"Nurzhan, what will I tell my friends when you come to the dance?"

"Don't worry. I thought about that problem. You will tell them you must baby-sit for me," he explained.

"But at a dance?"

"I think it will work. At least it is better than to say I am your chaperone."

"That is true."

Maya watched the orange light of the Mini-Mart sign blink on and off and heard Nurzhan's slow breathing as he fell asleep.

"Thank you, Nurzhan," she whispered and began to dream of the dance.

The next day Maya gave Mr. Horswill her permission slip and told him she had to baby-sit for her little brother. Maya asked him if Nurzhan could walk over from

Evergreen and stay in the gym until the dance was over, then they'd catch the bus together.

"I'll make a note of that," Mr. Horswill said. "We're not really set up to have elementary school people at our after-school events, but I think we can make an exception since you missed the skating party, Maya."

All that week and into the next, Shannon and Maya talked about the dance. Shannon talked about Kevin, but it didn't matter to Maya that there wasn't a special boy she wanted to dance with. Maya was just thrilled that she could go. And every night when Nurzhan watched TV after finishing his work, Maya practiced dancing in her room—just in case a boy did ask her to dance.

Shannon told Maya that her sisters advised her to ask the guys to dance. She said they explained that most guys are too shy to ask, so the girls need do it.

"I don't know if I could," Shannon said, as they rode to school the day before the dance. "Could you?"

"It would take much courage and I don't think I have such courage," Maya said.

"But my sisters insist it's the way to go. They said that you break the ice by asking the guys to dance and then after they dance once, they're not so afraid so they ask you."

"It sounds quite right if only a girl could be so brave."

"They also told me never under any circumstances to say 'no' to a boy who asks you to dance. Even a dork."

"Really? Why is that?"

"They said it takes so much nerve for the boys to ask that if you say 'no' they'll never ask you again. And the other guys will see this and be afraid you'd say 'no' to them and so they won't ask. Guys will never ask you again if you say 'no' to just one."

"You have much good fortune to have sisters to tell you these things."

"Yes, but now we both know."

The morning of the dance, while Maya and Nurzhan were eating kasha, Mama came into the kitchen. Mama still had a wrap on her ankle but she was walking much better now. She was happier and Maya could tell she felt better. It was better for her, too. When Mama was happier, Maya didn't feel so worried about her.

"Maya, I have something for you." Mama came to the table and put a small package wrapped in tissue paper in front of her. "Open." She pointed at the package.

Surprised, Maya looked up at her mother.

"Open."

Maya carefully unfolded the tissue paper and let out a gasp when she saw a small gold bracelet lying on the folds of the thin paper.

"You wear this to the dance." Mama patted her shoulder.

"Oh Mama." Maya wanted to hug her like they hug on

the gymnastics team but she didn't. In her family no one hugged like that.

"I forget sometimes when there is so much work that you are just a young girl," her mother said with a sigh. "This bracelet my mother gave to me when I was sixteen. Girls and boys dance younger here, Maya. So you wear this now."

"Thank you, Mama. I will be careful with it."

"I know. You're a good girl. And Nurzhan will be right there."

"Yes, Mama." Nurzhan nodded.

Shannon and Maya met in the bathroom after school and Shannon loaned Maya her peach lip gloss. Maya had her hair styled the way she had fixed it for the skating party and she wore the same outfit, too.

Nurzhan was waiting by the gym door when they got out of the bathroom. Shannon and Maya said "hi" to him and he followed them into the gym. Nurzhan found a chair next to the door and he waved to them while they joined Marcia Egness and Maria Flores—girls Shannon knew—and Dana Illo and Catherine Johnson from the gymnastics team. The gym got more and more crowded and everywhere you looked there were flocks of boys and flocks of girls, but no boys and girls together, as if they were birds that only stayed with their own kind.

Then a few eighth-grade guys and girls danced together. Faith Reeves and Antonio Warner, and Ruth Kumagai and Jonathan Bird and they were very cool and everyone watched them except some sixth-grade boys who were pushing each other across the floor in an large plastic garbage can.

Shannon turned to Maya, "I just remembered the other advice my sister gave me."

"What is this advice?"

"She said boys won't come up to a group of girls, so if you want to get asked to dance, you should stand alone."

"But it is not fun to do that," Maya said.

"Hey, Maya, see that guy?" Shannon asked, as she pointed to a group of guys near the garbage can with the sixth graders in it.

"Yes. I know him."

"I thought so. He's the guy that asked about you at the skating party. Who is he?"

"Tyler Lee. He's in my health class. I thought you said he was invisible."

"I just meant he doesn't stand out, he's not popular or anything, that's all. It doesn't mean he's creeper or anything. But listen, take my sister's advice. Ask him to dance," Shannon prodded.

Maya shook her head. "Oh no. I do not have courage."

"Okay, so leave our group and go stand by Nurzhan when the next song starts."

"I don't know, Shannon."

"Just do it. And then I'll go stand by him for the next song," Shannon whispered.

"Shannon, I think you should stand by Nurzhan first."

"He's your brother." Shannon laughed, as she shrugged her shoulders. "Oh well, okay. I'll do it."

When the next song started Shannon walked across the gym and stood by Nurzhan, who sat on the chair like a little mouse in the corner. Maya couldn't believe it, but it only took a few minutes before Kevin went over there and the next thing she knew Kevin and Shannon were dancing. They danced right by Maya and Shannon called out, "You're next, Maya!"

Maya's heart pounded as the song ended and she walked across the gym. She could feel the red flushing her cheeks with her borscht face and she found Soldat to walk with her across the gym. As she got near Nurzhan's chair Maya saw Daniel Moran and Nadine Slodky dancing, so Mrs. Roosevelt joined her, too.

"No one can make you feel inferior without your permission, Maya."

"I do not give permission, Mrs. Roosevelt." Maya said,

glancing at Daniel and Nadine as she went to her brother. "Hi, Nurzhan."

"Hi."

"Are you doing okay?" she asked.

"Yes. It's a little boring though."

"I'm sorry you have to be here."

"It's not that bad. The boys in the garbage can are fun to watch. I would enjoy doing that if I came to this dance."

Nurzhan and Maya talked some more but she felt dumb standing there by herself away from the other girls. She was beginning to think that Shannon's sister's advice could only work for Shannon and it could never work for her, when out of the corner of her eye she saw a guy coming toward her. It was Tyler.

"Dance?" Tyler asked.

"Sure." Maya smiled. She was so happy to see him even though she was embarrassed about her face, which she knew was the deepest red—although Maya noticed that Tyler's ears were red, too.

Tyler held her hand and put his arm around her waist and she put her hand on his shoulder just the way Shannon and Maya had practiced so many times. It was a slow dance and Mama's bracelet gleamed on her hand as it lay on Tyler's shoulder. Tyler and Maya talked a little and then he teased her in a gentle way.

"How's the horse eater?"

"Great. How are you, chicken toe?"

Then they laughed and then they were quiet and danced even more slowly and Tyler moved a little closer to her. Maya looked over, afraid that Nurzhan was watching and would have to report to Mama and Papa—but all she saw was an empty chair. And then they danced even closer.

Tyler and Maya danced four more times that afternoon (two fast and two *very* slow) and each time Nurzhan's chair was empty and he seemed to have disappeared. Maya didn't think too much about Nurzhan during the rest of the dance, and on the bus going home, while Shannon and Maya talked and talked, re-living every wonderful moment, she almost forgot he was there.

But that night when Nurzhan and Maya were going to sleep and she was thinking about how it had been the best day of her life, she thanked Nurzhan for making it possible for her to go to the dance.

"There's just one thing I wondered about," Maya whispered as the Mini-Mart sign blinked on and off.

"What's that?"

"Where did you go when I danced with Tyler?"

"To wait in the bathroom. So I could tell Mama and Papa with truth that I saw nothing."

"The bathroom?"

"Yes."

"You are an excellent chaperone."

Nurzhan and Maya giggled so loud Mama came in and told them to be quiet. "Shhh, Nurzhan, Maya. Go to sleep!" She spoke sharply to both of them.

After Mama left and closed their door, Maya sat up. "Thank you again, Nurzhan," Maya whispered.

"Sure."

"Goodnight," she said softly, snuggling back down under the covers.

"Goodnight, Maya."

Nurzhan fell asleep right away like he usually did. But Maya lay awake for a while and looked at the table by her bed and saw the gold bracelet shining in the blinking light of the Mini-Mart sign and she imagined Mama wearing it when she was sixteen and Maya treasured what she'd said as much as the bracelet. "Girls and boys dance younger here, Maya. So you wear this now."

And Maya thought of Tyler, who Shannon said was not popular, but Maya knew was a person with a good heart. She wasn't sure if she was ready for a real boyfriend, but Tyler was a special friend who was a boy—dancing with him had been a very fun and cool thing. *Kak zamechatel'no.* How wonderful. Chicken toe…horse eater. It made her laugh inside and she decided right then to tell Soldat that he could play with his dog friends. They could sniff each other and chase around and do dog things, because she didn't need him quite so much. I have my brother and we help each other, she thought, as she yawned.

Maya glanced over again at Nurzhan. I might not even need Mrs. Roosevelt so often, she thought with a smile. Then she closed her eyes, hoping very much that Nurzhan would like to chaperone at the next dance.

GLOSSARY

Glossary of Words and Phrases used in *Maya and the Cotton Candy Boy*

Beshbarmak: stew-like soup with noodles, meat, potatoes and onion

Chto: what

Eto normal'no: it's okay

Idi Syuda: come here

Kak zamechatel'no: how wonderful

Kamcha: whip

Nichego: nothing

Nyet: no

Ostanovit: stop

Prizrak: ghost

Prosti menya: forgive me

Soldat: soldier

Spravka: help

Tenge: currency of Kazakhstan

Ya tebya ne vinyu: I don't blame you

ABOUT THE AUTHOR

JEAN DAVIES OKIMOTO is the recipient of the ALA Best Book for Young Adults Award, the Parents' Choice Award, the Green Earth Book Award and is the author of two Smithsonian Notable Books. She and her husband Joe live on Vashon Island near Seattle, Washington. She can be contacted through her website www.jeandaviesokimoto.com. Additionally, an excellent resource about bullying can be found at www.bulliesinbooks.com.

LaVergne, TN USA
11 April 2011
223735LV00003B/13/P